The Last Christmas

A Novel

Dale J. Moore

The Last Christmas / Dale J. Moore - 1st Edition Trade Paperback

ISBN 978-1-0689823-6-1

This book and others by Northern Amusements are available in electronic format. Visit our web site at www.northernamusements.com.

e-Pub version
ISBN 978-1-0689823-7-8

Cover by Dale J. Moore
Edited by Maureen P. Moore
Printed and bound in Canada and/or the United States.

Dedications

To my family, siblings, and in-laws. May we get through the tough times ahead with dignity and grace. And remember, this is fiction.

Table of Contents

December 19th

1   *Breakfast*

Elizabeth Margaret Montgomery slowly sat up, her short silver-grey hair barely moving while she rotated her hips to sit uncomfortably at the edge of the king-size bed. Her feet dangled above the floor. This was the worst part, she told herself. Age continued to take its toll on her now eighty-seven-year-old frame. From her perspective, she was happy to still be breathing and somewhat mobile, having lost too many dear people in her life over the past ten years. She took a deep breath and exhaled before cautiously wiggling her butt toward the edge of the bed. Her hands tightly gripped the rim of the mattress, like grasping the ledge of a cliff. One final lower body nudge and her feet found the slip-proof slippers awaiting their return. Her backside leaned tightly against the bed as she carefully slid each foot into place. Lizzie, as her closest friends called her, leaned forward to tug her handbrake-locked shiny red walker closer for the transition from sitting to standing. She jokingly referred to her walker as the 'Red Flash', carrying the nickname of her late husband's muscle car from the sixties. The walker lacked the yellow flames on the side. The only motor was her withering legs, but it got her where she needed to go. Which at this moment was the kitchen

table. The rousing aromas of Maura's wonderful hot breakfast added motivation to get out of bed unaided this morning.

As she slowly walked down the glistening hardwood hallway from her transplanted bedroom, she recalled putting up a fuss about moving out of the second floor grand master. Until the first slip and fall. She never let onto her children how much pain, or damage, that tumble had caused, from bruised hips and knees to a small fracture in her left hand. With her children spread all over Canada, she could conceal the injuries from them. They never visited. Scratch that – they hardly ever visited.

A year ago, when Maura threatened to leave if her employer remained on the second floor, Lizzie reluctantly relented. Lizzie quickly came to realize it was the smart thing to do, though she immensely missed her cultured-stone-surrounded master bedroom fireplace. She missed the performance of the dancing gas flames as she snuggled into bed to read. A convenient remote doused the flames once the warmth enveloped her bed sufficiently to keep her cozy until she laid her book down for the night. Lizzie had a contractor lined up to install a smaller replica of her old fireplace in her current bedroom, but he was booked well into the new year. She could have gotten another contractor, but Jordan was the son of a late dear high school friend.

Nearing the kitchen, she scanned the area for Maura, knowing she wasn't far from the enticing scents.

"Bom Dia, Maura," she called out to her mid-thirties single Portuguese maid, personal support worker, confidante, and now, likely her best friend.

"Bom Dia, Lizzie," she replied, appearing from the dining room smiling. "I was dusting the hutch. Those adorable Rinconada animal figurines don't dust themselves." She grinned and started to remove her elbow-length gloves. "I have French toast and bacon for you this morning."

"Wonderful!" Lizzie replied, her still youthful blue eyes flashing the happiness of a child seeing a breakfast buffet for the first time.

"Give me a minute and I'll get it off the stove."

"I can get it," Lizzie told her. "I'm right here. I'm not completely helpless, you know," she grinned at Maura.

"I know but let me do it," Maura implored over her shoulder, stepping into the dining room to lay down her gloves. "The pans are still hot," she called from around the corner. "I just turned them off a minute ago."

Before Maura could step out of the dining room, Lizzie pushed her way up to the stove. She grabbed a plate from the counter and placed it on the empty burner beside the bacon. Then she speared a slice of French toast with a fork. She shook the toast off the fork. It landed on the plate, the bottom crust overhanging the gold gilded edge. Close enough, she thought. Next, she turned her attention to the bacon. She deftly slid the fork under three slices of bacon, turning her upper body slightly. The greasy bacon dripped from the fork as it hung between the frying pan and her plate. As she turned back, her balance left her. The hot bacon slid down the fork onto her right hand. She screamed at the pain of the bubbling grease burning her flesh. She grabbed for the walker with her left hand but, blinded by pain, she missed the grip, her hand instead plunging down on the end of the handle of the scalding cast iron frying pan. The metal pan flipped into the air, the hot grease, bacon, and pan searing her face as she tumbled to the ground. She screamed like she'd never screamed before, instinctively grabbing for her face and spreading the hot grease in the process. She collapsed in a rumpled heap within the railings of her walker.

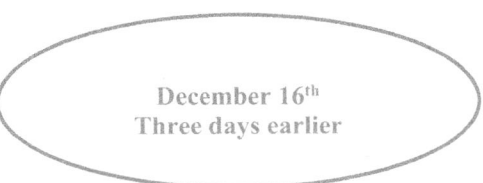

December 16th
Three days earlier

2 Danny Miller

The navy blue 1995 Mustang Fastback pulled into the Montgomery driveway with no concern for the leaking oil pan. Inside, Danny Miller checked his hair in the mirror, looking for perfection. Unhappy, he grabbed a travel size hair spray and gave the combed-over top a fresh hold. He impulsively checked his teeth with a stretched smile, like an eight-year-old awkwardly posing for school day pictures. He ignored the obvious ugly scar running from the corner of his right eye to his right ear. Satisfied with his appearance, Danny opened the car door and slid out, tugging on the bottom of his suitcoat as he stood. Straightening the shoulders of the jacket covering his six-foot-two-inch frame, he proceeded up the melted driveway, admiring the job done automatically by the built-in snow melting system. It seemed like magic. *I got to get that done next year.* He put a hand on his often aching back, denying that the fifty plus pounds hanging over his belt at the front were the cause; he preferred to attribute the pain to shovelling and other heavy lifting.

He looked around the front yard. On top of the light snow covering the grass lay a bunch of deflated Christmas lawn inflatables. He lost track trying to count the colourful lumps on the ground, though he was sure it was more than last year. He hated the miserable things, likely due to his dislike of Christmas itself. He resented that his sister always seemed to get more stuff than him when they were young. He sat firmly in the 'Bah Humbug' club.

He did, however, love this house. Not as much as the original Montgomery house, still he'd love to own a place like this. It said class – just like him, he thought. The chicks would love to come back to a place like this. They'd beg him for it once they set their eyes on this place, that's for sure. He sighed, thinking about his small two-bedroom wartime house. His sister got the old man's place when he croaked. He took ownership of the used car dealership. He felt that he came out ahead overall, which was the most important thing to him. Winning a deal was the number one rule that guided his life.

He reached the front-door landing and rang the doorbell. He cursed to himself when the musical bell rang. He hated gimmicky doorbells on homes, especially Christmas ones. He loved the one he'd installed at the dealership that played when someone opened an exterior door. 'Sell, Sell, Sell' by the Barenaked Ladies. He always thought of himself as clever that way.

The front door opened, revealing the Montgomery's maid. He had a thing for Mexican women.

"Buenos nachos, Maria. Still as hot as a tamale, I have to say." He leered over the woman.

Maura stared at him, never sure what to say. Any response would likely encourage him. She looked at herself, wearing sweatpants and matching top, her hair tied up in a bow stuffed inside a hair bonnet.

Her arms were covered in long rubber gloves she used for cleaning the toilets. 'Hot' was not a good description for her current appearance.

"You want to see the boss lady?" she asked flatly, minimizing eye contact.

"Maybe you could do something for me with those rubber gloves first," he grinned creepily.

"Like slap you silly?" Maura asked.

"Oooo," moaned Danny. "I could go for a little domination, Master Maria." He rubbed his crotch.

She rolled her eyes, right about any remark encouraging him. "Let me get Mrs. Montgomery for you."

"Cool. Just walk slowly. I want to watch that wonderful wiggle of yours," Danny laughed.

Maura shook her head. She tried to walk as un-sexy as possible before she disappeared down the hallway. A minute later, Lizzie appeared trailing Maura, an envelope clutched between her left hand and the grip of her walker.

"Afternoon, Mrs. M," Danny said. "I was just telling your Mexican maid here what a beautiful sunny day it is today."

"She's Portuguese," Lizzie replied.

"I don't care where in Mexico she's from, unless we hook up and I have to go there or something." He stepped through the doorway into the foyer, looking around at the wood adorning the house, then finally up at the large glistening chandelier overhead. "This sure is a nice place that your late husband provided for you." He looked back at Mrs. Montgomery, a devilish grin on his face. "Just like he said he'd provide for me." He suggestively touched his scar.

"Here's your money." She started to hand it to him, then abruptly pulled it back. "But this is the last one. This has gone on for twenty years. I'm tired of your extortion. I've paid you about a quarter of a million. Enough is enough."

"Yeah, you're right." He lunged forward and ripped the envelope out of her hand. He shoved it in his front suitcoat pocket. Mrs. Montgomery staggered from his sudden action. She quickly secured her footing, though flush from the surprise. He quickly turned, grabbing Maura by the rubber covering her wrist and yanking her forcefully into his grasp. With Maura's neck in the crook of his elbow and facing Lizzie, Danny's eyes glared with wicked intent. He uttered new demands through gritted teeth. "I don't think so, Mommy dearest." He thrust his hips against the captive Maura. "In fact, I may make your sweet Mexican black-eyed beauty squeal with delight right here in front of you, unless you give me an extra grand next week." He grinned evilly. "Let's call it a Christmas bonus, shall we? A sign of good faith that the payments will continue." He laughed a throaty 'hey, hey, hey'.

"Ugh!" Mrs. Montgomery exclaimed. "You're a horrible man. I don't know what she ever saw in you!"

"She saw my potential, is what she saw. Too bad she didn't stick around to see the shrewd businessman I am today." He laughed his ugly laugh again, roughly pushing Maura to the ground in front of Mrs. Montgomery. "I'll see you in a week. The twenty-third. Have my Christmas bonus ready or else…" He sneered at them, then yelled "Boo!", causing the women to flinch. He laughed again and turned for the door. Holding up his left hand as he walked onto the porch, he waved and called out "Later."

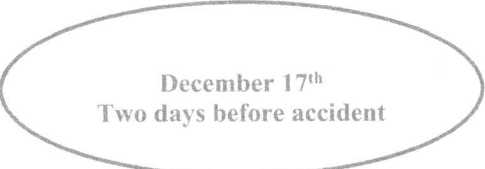

December 17th
Two days before accident

3 The Weekly Calls - Kevin

Two days before her accident, Mrs. Montgomery conducted her weekly calls to her children from her home in LaSalle, Ontario. Maura had helped her set up the video on her smart device about six months prior. Having sent each of her children a paired device, they made weekly calls around noon each Sunday. At least noon their time. That meant eleven a.m. for her call to her second oldest, Kevin, who lived in Cape Breton, Nova Scotia. An hour later, she called her middle child, Ron, in Toronto. The second youngest, Mark, had set up in Calgary close to thirty years earlier, while the youngest, Heather, lived in Prince Rupert up the coast of British Columbia.

She'd pleaded with each of her children in early September to come home for Christmas, hoping sufficient advance notice might spur them to make plans. Instead, she got more excuses than Ron had used when he'd broken Mark's arm as a teenager. She'd moved on, dejected in the knowledge that it was ten years this Christmas since any of them had set foot in her home for the holiday. Only Heather had visited her home at all during that time. Not their home, as her children would remind her. Two years after her husband Bill had passed on, she sold the 'family' home and downsized to the smaller monstrosity she currently called home. She didn't need eight thousand square feet with a four-car garage and three acres of lawn to maintain – or at least pay to have maintained. The new house was still far beyond her space needs. She had envisioned frequent visits from her kids and grandkids and wanted to have extra bedrooms for that eventuality. She sighed at the original thought, realizing it was a fruitless pursuit, her children's roots replanted in places spread around their immense and diverse country.

"Good morning, Kevin!" she smiled at the screen. Her son's heavily bearded face smiled back at her. She preferred his face clean-shaven instead of the grey-specked abomination that she felt hid his good looks.

"Hi, Mom. Nice to see you."

"You look good, Kevin. What's new?" Behind her son she could see his snow and fir tree-covered backyard that resembled a classic Christmas card.

"Charlotte's off to see the grandkids play hockey, then they're back here with their parents for dinner tonight."

She watched him sip on his steaming coffee, by the looks of it freshly poured for this call. The coffee looked so good she could almost smell it through the screen. "Remember those days when you played?" Her six-foot son was a good athlete in his younger days but carried about twenty extra pounds these days.

"Oh yeah. I don't know how you shuttled us all around to activities, with Dad on the road so much."

"In fairness, your father did cart the lot of you around on weekends whenever he could. And once Mary got her driver's licence, she helped with Mark and Heather."

Kevin caught his breath. He always did at the mention of his late sister. "I think she did that so I couldn't have the car once I got my licence." He tried to muster a laugh.

"Maybe, dear," his mother replied. "She did like the freedom that driving brought her when she was young."

"I suppose," her son replied. "I just found it ironic that she stopped driving when she reached her forties."

"She got into the 'save the planet' stuff long before most of us took it seriously."

"I guess she had to save something else after saving me," Kevin reflected.

His mother forced a smile, remembering a painful episode in their family's history. Her son had worked in downtown Toronto at the Stock Exchange for over three years. By all outward impressions he was highly successful. His lifestyle though was one of reckless abandon. His health began plummeting like a stock after a scandal. His mental health hung by a thread. He'd taken to 'supplements', as he'd described them to her at the time, to stay 'focused and alert'. They were addictive narcotics. He'd come home for a long weekend at Christmas one year, with yet another new girlfriend in tow. Lizzie had lost track. She took to writing their names on the palm of her hand to avoid calling them the wrong name during phone calls or visits. His girlfriends that she met mostly seemed like nice young women; however, they quickly tired of her son's misbehaviour and unhealthy habits. She remembered how this girlfriend pulled Mary aside that Christmas for a 'girl to girl' talk about Kevin's problems. Mary devised a plan where they knocked out her younger brother by drugging the booze he used to wash down his 'magic helpers'. It took hours for it to take effect. When it did, the two young women wondered if they had killed Kevin, his heartbeat so slow it was barely discernible. They took advantage of his unconscious state and forged his signature to check him into a substance abuse retreat. Kevin remained in the clinic for two weeks, until Mary visited and agreed to his release. He claimed those were the two most difficult weeks of his life. When he came out, he was a new man, ready for change. He knew a change in lifestyle, job, and location were required to keep from reverting to old habits. He quit his job in Toronto and moved with his girlfriend, and future wife, Charlotte, back to her hometown in Nova Scotia, taking a much less stressful job as a financial planner. He'd stayed clean since, leaning on Charlotte a lot in the first few months to keep him from slipping. Every year he had bought Mary a special Christmas ornament as a reminder thank you.

"Oh, before I forget." She snapped out of her reminiscence. "I shipped off the bundle of Christmas gifts to the lot of you on Friday. You should get them in time for Christmas. I'll have Maura send you the tracking number, though she'll keep an eye on it."

"If it's anything like last year, they'll have to dedicate a truck to haul your presents out here." He half smiled. "You really need to cut back on it, Mom. We don't need that much, nor do the kids. Just send to their kids next year, okay?"

His mother sighed. "You know how much I love Christmas. I like shopping for all of you."

"Yeah, but does Maura?" He cut to the chase. "I'm sure she's doing most of it by now."

She blushed. "Maybe she's doing some of it." She could hear Maura laugh in the background. "Okay, yes, Maura is doing most of it. I can't get around the mall anymore. I feel like I'm going to get run over by kids or mall walkers. I buy some stuff by myself online. I enjoy that."

"Well, instead of having them ship it to your house, have them send it directly here. It will save time and money."

"That's what Maura says. But I won't get to see the gifts or wrap them if I send them directly. I might as well just send everyone money," she said, exasperated.

"There is nothing wrong with sending money."

"It's impersonal, is what it is. And how do I know you will spend the money on presents? Maybe you'll blow it on booze!"

Kevin laughed. "Wrong child, mother. I was the one on speed."

"I'm sorry," she frowned, regretting she'd brought up the past. "Remember how Mark would open his card from your grandmother, proudly hold up the twenty-dollar bill, and proclaim, 'a gift of money', waving it around for everyone to see."

"Yeah, he still does that I think." Kevin laughed. "I better get going, Mom. I hear a car in the driveway. Talk to you soon."

He hung up abruptly, cutting her off from saying goodbye, or asking him to hang on to see her granddaughter and her kids. She wiped a tear from her eye, readying herself for her next call at the top of the hour.

17

Dale J. Moore

December 19th
Day of accident

4   *Emergency Room*

The paramedics arrived quickly, though it seemed like an eternity for Maura. She'd never felt so helpless. While waiting, she tried to make Lizzie comfortable by cooling her skin with cold water. She stopped when some skin became loose and flaky. She wanted to hold her friend's hand to soothe her. The burns were simply too bad on her frail hands. Instead, Maura gently placed a hand on Lizzie's arm, an area she could see had escaped the ravages of the grease.

Maura described the accident to the paramedics and stepped back, hands cupped over her mouth. Tears streamed down her cheeks onto her fingers. They medicated and prepared her boss for transport to the hospital, apprising Maura of the receiving hospital. They advised her to get someone to drive her if she still suffered from shock. Maura nodded instinctively, blanking out on every detail they provided after the hospital name.

An hour later, Maura sat in a protective gown, gloves, and mask at the emergency triage bed next to her friend, who slept under a protective canopy, mercifully sedated. Maura kicked herself for not stopping Lizzie. Sure, the woman had served herself many times in the past, but she shouldn't have let her today. Why did she let her today? It was only a matter of time before something like this would happen. Maura knew Lizzie was slowly degrading in her motor skills. She thought it was a year or more away from becoming serious. She beat herself up inside, saying she should have known better. She was a trained personal support worker, after all. Sure, she hadn't worked in a long-term care facility in over five years due to the anxiety attacks that left her running for air and space. But she knew better. She knew better, she repeated over and over in her mind. She'd let her friendship with her boss impact her judgement. It was clearly her fault this happened. Neglect, they called it. She'd have to resign immediately. That was the only solution. Not that it would roll back time nor heal her friend. That she'd have to live with, employed by Mrs. Montgomery or not.

Shortly, a nurse came around to prepare to wheel Mrs. Montgomery away. "We're moving her to an isolation room to better protect her from infection. That is the most serious threat right now. Any infection would jeopardize her healing process. You'll have to leave now. Check back in the morning if you'd like." The nurse paused, putting a comforting gloved hand on Maura's shoulder. She looked sympathetically into Maura's eyes. "It's going to be a long road to recovery, judging from the extent of her burns and her age. You should go home. Get some sleep. Take something to help you sleep, if needed. You look exhausted."

Maura nodded, wiping a fresh batch of tears from her face. She tried saying thank you, but her voice cracked and failed her. Just as she'd failed Lizzie.

December 17th
Two days before accident

5 The Weekly Calls - Ron

Continuing her calls two days before the accident, Mrs. Montgomery connected with her middle child, Ron, at his condo in Toronto.

"Hello, Mother," Ron said as the connection kicked in. "How are you today?"

"I'm good, son. So is Kevin. Just spoke with him." She could see the large glass windows of his downtown condo reflecting the sun in the background. Between glimmers of sun, she could see several other towers through the glass. He lived on the twenty-second floor with his wife.

"I bet he's busy with that gaggle of grandkids he has."

She smiled. "Yes, it keeps them running to activities, and busy with babysitting of course." She studied the lines on her son's face. Just past his mid-fifties, his age was showing, from the creases adorning his facial features to his greying, though touched-up black hair. "How have you and Sharon been?"

"I'm busy as usual. Have a couple of condo showings after this call. Sunday is one of my busiest days, at least for showings. It's great to be busy when you're a real estate broker."

"Great commissions I suppose."

"And it's even better as a broker and getting a cut from other people's work. Dad always said a smart man lets other people do the heavy lifting for him, while he focuses on growing the business."

"Your father was a good businessman. He travelled a lot to grow the business. He made a point to treat his employees well too."

A wide grin lit up Ron's face. "Then you'll feel happy with what I'm about to tell you."

"What's that?"

"We've had such a good year that I'm giving Christmas bonuses to all my employees, ranging from Caribbean vacations for our top sellers to weeklong getaways to my cottage in Muskoka for other agents."

"You didn't forget about the hard working office staff, did you?"

He laughed. "I knew you'd ask about them. Wasn't it you that told dad that they are the glue that holds a company together?"

"Something like that," she laughed. "I'm glad you remembered."

"The office staff are getting five-hundred-dollar gift cards, and an extra three paid vacation days next year."

"Your father would be proud," she smiled, holding back a tear. "I bet that extra time off will mean a lot to the office staff."

"Thanks, Mom. That's what they told me they wanted most – more time off."

Changing topics, his mother asked, "How's Sharon doing?"

"She's done some amazing work recently redecorating some high-end waterfront condos. I'll have her send you some pictures."

"I'd love that, thank you. You know how much I enjoy seeing her masterpieces. She made a good choice changing careers."

Ron shuffled in his seat. "She was a good real estate agent, but I agree, she's much happier now. She enjoys selling her ideas, instead of trying to sell someone else's property." He paused, fidgeting.

"What is it, Ron?"

"You know, I never saw it." He leaned forward in his chair. "I never saw she wasn't happy. Looking back, I can see she was becoming less cheerful and more distant. I really might have lost her if ..."

His mother finished for him. "If not for Mary? Is that what you were going to say?"

He silently nodded.

"That sister of yours had a way of seeing into people's souls, I think. I remember that Christmas very well. Mary had just published her first book and it was taking off. None of that mattered to her. In fact, she didn't even mention it until Mark saw it on the best sellers list."

"Yeah, she was like that. Always helping other people, without bragging about her own successes." He smiled at his mother. "You know I could never keep my successes to myself."

"I hadn't noticed," she laughed. "Back to Sharon. I think it was two days before Christmas. You guys arrived earlier in the day. Mary picked up on something the moment she greeted Sharon. I remember sitting with her and Sharon by the fire that night, having a hot chocolate."

"With Bailey's," Ron added.

"Of course! Extra in mine," his mother grinned. "I remember Sharon confided in Mary that she was afraid of losing you if she quit the real estate business. After all, you had just started your own brokerage and were struggling a bit."

"I remember those days. I had some doubts the brokerage would succeed. There was a lot of competition – even more now."

"Well, Mary simply asked Sharon what she'd rather do with her life. Sharon quickly said interior design. She'd taken it in school. She felt it helped her with staging houses, which led to more offers and more sales. Mary stood up, moving her arm around, pointing at the room. She asked Sharon what she'd do to the room to make it more appealing to a prospective buyer, or even for visitors, for that matter. Sharon slowly stood, studying the room. I remember glancing around and thinking 'what's wrong with this room?' she smiled. "Sharon described how she would rearrange the furniture, get rid of the rug to bring out the colour of the hardwood underneath, change the colour scheme to match the revealed floor, and replace the curtains with something that allowed additional light into the room. That was just the start. The two of them headed out the next morning to get what she needed, down to trinkets to put on the tables. I can imagine them now, on Christmas Eve day scurrying around to all these stores in the morning and transforming the room prior to dinner. Sharon sure proved me wrong about the room. The transformation was magnificent. It was like a new room. Like a room from Better Homes and Gardens."

"Yes, it was. After dinner, Sharon pulled me aside in the foyer. She gave me her notice she was quitting real estate sales. I was stunned at first, not sure what to say. I held her hands and stared at her, speechless. Then I saw it. I saw a renewed energy emitting from everywhere on her face. She almost glowed. The light had returned to her eyes."

"She gave you a month's notice, if I remember."

Ron laughed. "Yeah, she gave me time to find a replacement. She'd already lined up customers for her new business before the month was up. She had transformed."

His mother smiled. "The caterpillar had become a butterfly."

Ron's grin devolved into a sad pout. "I really miss Mary at this time of year," Ron quietly stated, fighting his emotions. He quickly checked his watch. "Mom, I've got to go – clients are waiting! Talk to you next week."

She watched him lean forward to disconnect the call, wiping a tear from his cheek with the back of his other hand.

Dale J. Moore

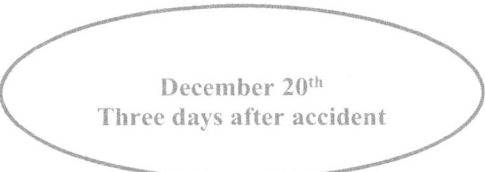

6 The Hospital

"Sit down please," Dr. Raymond told Maura, motioning to a large winged-back chair in front of his desk.

Maura sat nervously, her thumbs moving continuously over her intertwined hands.

The doctor looked at the fidgeting Maura. "First, I want to thank you for your quick action in summoning 911 and giving the paramedics a detailed description of the incident."

Maura nodded thank you.

He looked down to open a folder in front of him, exposing a report. "Mrs. Montgomery has burns of varying severity. Her face has first-degree burns, meaning the burn isn't deep but it's likely excruciatingly painful. She's under constant medication to manage her pain." He looked up for acknowledgement.

Maura looked down, quietly sobbing.

The doctor paused for a minute. He read more from his report. "Her right hand has a severe third-degree burn on the top and will take considerable treatment. Her left hand has a small third-degree burn between the thumb and index finger that will make it painful to grip anything for some time. She has a few other burns from splatter.

Nothing serious on their own." Again, he looked up at Maura. "Questions?"

"What's the recovery time for this, Doctor?"

He closed the file in front of him. "It is difficult to predict, especially with elderly patients. As I'm sure you are aware, we don't heal nearly as quickly as we age. On the bright side, she is in good health and, as you've said, her mind is sharp." He paused and stood up, straightening his white lab coat. "I must be frank with you. Sometimes the biggest challenge we have with octogenarians is their will to live and fight to get better. They often find it difficult to have a purpose to go on. They really must want to live. That's where you come in."

"Me?" questioned Maura.

"Yes, you." The doctor removed his reading glasses, placing them down softly. He crossed his arms, looking intently across the table. "Once she is out of isolation, you need to talk to her every day, or better yet, have her family come by frequently to remind her of her reasons to live. She'll be bandaged. That will reduce the visible shock to all of you, somewhat anyway."

"I'm afraid her family is spread all over the country. They haven't come to visit her in ten years."

Dr. Raymond took a deep, thoughtful breath. He leaned forward, placing a hand on his desk. "That's unfortunate, really unfortunate." His eyebrows narrowed; his tone turned serious. "You need to convince them to come or else do the heavy lifting of visiting by yourself. I recommend you reach out, explain the situation. It is exhausting to keep up a solo vigil. Don't sugarcoat the severity of her injuries when you call them. Explain that this is serious. They need to be here. All of them, if possible."

Maura nodded.

"One more thing," he added. "She won't be able to talk, nor will she be able to move. She'll be medicated and restrained to prevent injuring herself. It will be a one-way conversation. After a while she may get the strength to nod."

"I understand. I will do my best to get her family here." Maura still looked down at her restless hands.

"Look up, Maura," he asked her. She complied. "That's great, but not good enough. As a famous philosopher once said, 'Try not. Do. Or do not. There is no try."

Maura cracked a small grin. "Are you quoting Yoda?"

"Yes," he grinned back. "Sadly, their mother's life may depend on you doing, not trying."

Maura sucked in a deep breath, that statement rattling her. She didn't know if she could succeed. Lizzie had tried for ten years to get them to visit.

The doctor continued. "We'll keep her in isolation a bit longer. We go by the rule of nines for estimating the amount of burn to the body. Nine percent for her head, and nine percent for each hand. If I stuck strictly to that rule, I'd say twenty-seven percent coverage for Mrs. Montgomery. However, with the varying degree of burns and the size of the impacted areas, I'm going to cut that to ten percent. We generally estimate a half day for each percent. That would mean five days in isolation, give or take on her progress. Taking into account the time since the accident, you should tell her children to get here in two or three days. We should see enough progress by then to move her to her own room. The antibiotics will begin to fight off the risk of infection by then as well." He sat back down. "Any questions?" He waited. "Okay, I'm sure you're still in shock. Here's my card. Call and leave a message. I'm often busy and can't answer directly. I will call back or have a nurse respond with an update."

Maura stood up and hesitantly took the card, looking at it momentarily then sliding it into the outside pocket of her purse. She looked up, trails of dried tears on her face. "Thank you, Doctor."

"You're welcome."

She turned for the door.

"And Maura," he said, causing her to stop and turn around. "This wasn't your fault. If anything, your actions have reduced her pain and improved her chance of recovery. Keep that in mind, please."

She nodded, a broken smile covering the guilt she still shouldered.

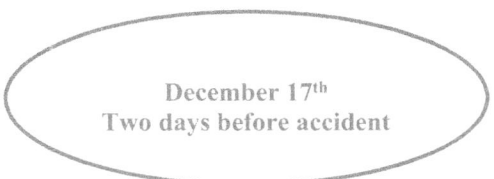

December 17th
Two days before accident

7 *The Weekly Calls - Mark*

Mark Montgomery awaited the call from his mother. Sitting in the office at the back of his house on a hill, he had a faint glimpse of the Calgary skyline from his suburban home. He'd already gotten past her annual call asking for his family to come for Christmas, and their conversations had moved on. His smart device chimed; he unconsciously straightened up in his chair to answer. Mrs. Montgomery had taught her children good posture at an early age, frequently reminding them during their ascent to adulthood.

"Good morning, Mom."

"Hello, Mark. How are you and the family doing?"

He relaxed at her warm smile. "Everyone's good. Patty and I are babysitting Maggie's youngest this weekend. Maggie and Jack took Jack Jr. to Banff for the weekend. The little guy is getting on skis for the first time."

"That's nice of you to take little Liza for them. I bet Jack Jr. will have a blast."

"I just hope they all come back in one piece." He paused, remembering Maggie's skiing accident when she was ten. He'd felt guilty for the entire time she bore that arm cast.

"If I remember correctly," his mother replied, knowing what her son was thinking, "Young Maggie wore that cast like a badge of honour."

Mark laughed. "I suppose you're right. But Jack Jr. is much younger."

"That just means he'll bounce back quicker if he gets hurt." She lamented for a moment. "I remember getting cuts and scratches crawling through the brush. They'd heal in a day. Now I wear those reminders for weeks before they fade away."

He smiled at her, paraphrasing an oft-said expression. "Yep, it's a bitch getting old, but it beats the alternative."

"You are right about that, son." She took a sip of her tea. "Since you've got Liza there, can I see her?"

"Sure, Mom. Give me a sec." He disappeared, leaving her to stare at the crowded bookshelf behind his desk. The books appeared mostly related to work; she recognized the construction books that had also resided on her husband's shelves. She grinned upon spotting Mary's work on the top shelf.

"Here we go, Mom." He sat down, holding a one-year-old tenderly on his lap. Liza wore a frilly seasonal dress, with a red velvet headband that she tried to flip off with her tiny wrinkly fingers. He could hear his mother sigh first, then begin baby prattle to her great-grandchild. The sight warmed his heart. He realized that his mother must miss doing this in person. "She's a cutie, isn't she?"

"She certainly is. She reminds me of Maggie, except her nose is yours."

"That's what I say!" he exclaimed. "Most people say Liza looks like her dad. I see a dead ringer for Maggie, except for the nose, like you say." He grinned, adjusting the baby's headband. "Funny that you see that too."

At that moment, the baby let out gas. Mark lifted her up, holding her at arms-length away from his crinkled up nose. "I better get her back to Patty. I think our angel just filled her diaper."

He could hear his mother chuckling as he once again briefly left the room. When he sat back down, he continued the conversation. "I'm glad you're on the line so I didn't have to change her. For someone so small, that Liza knows how to fill a diaper."

His mother laughed. "Mary was the smallest baby I had, but somehow she made a bigger mess in her diaper than any two of you combined."

Mark laughed at this new revelation. "Funny, I always thought Ron was the one full of shit." He meant it as a joke, but there was a history of issues between him and his closest-in-age brother. He awaited a scowl from his mother for his language. It never came, surprisingly.

"Only when he's trying to seal a real estate deal." She laughed at her own comment.

"Guess it's part of any job where you sell stuff. I've been known to embellish a bit selling new home builds."

"Your father must have taught you that," she replied, thinking of her late husband's very successful construction business.

"That and a world of other things. I wouldn't be where I'm at today without him."

"Or Mary," his mother added.

"Or Mary," he agreed, thinking back twenty or more years. His construction company teetered on bankruptcy back then. Taking out a few significant loans, he'd purchased a couple of large tracts of land in Calgary's suburbs, destined for high-end subdivisions. Then the current oil boom ended. The real estate market collapsed like a kid's house of cards. People couldn't afford their existing homes, let alone new ones. It was then that he made one of the worst mistakes of his life. He started doing cocaine to escape his problems. Small amounts at first. An attitude adjustment, he referred to it at the time, insisting it wasn't a habit, just a way to focus. As his problems grew his drug usage grew with them. Which only made everything worse. The depths of his fall came when he attended a meeting at city hall with a group of other property developers, seeking temporary tax relief for their vacant land. The council denied the motion. Mark, fuelled by a quick snort in the hallway at recess before the motion, completely lost it. He began screaming at the entire council. He then attacked the mayor, first verbally in a rant that made Clark Griswold's rant about his boss pale in comparison, then physically. He spent several painful withdrawal nights in jail sobering up, his wife refusing to bail him out in hopes he'd take a pause to reflect and rethink his lifestyle choices. He did. He sold off his personal toys, his Corvette and boat, but he was still broke. His wife's job kept food on the table for the time being. When he confided in his older sister Mary about his financial issues, she told him she'd lend him the money. Her latest book had done very well. She told him she was looking for an investment. She told him she had a hunch real estate would bounce back in a big way the following year. She wanted in while it was in a low phase.

"I don't know what would have happened if she didn't bail me out," he lamented.

"Or you bail her out," his mother replied.

Mark looked at her curiously. "What do you mean?"

"You never knew, did you?"

"Knew what?"

"She didn't have that kind of money. What Mary didn't tell you was that she took loans from five investors. She was paying them interest, including your father. And you know he *never* lent money to family. She convinced him to join the group of investors. She was up to her eyeballs in debt after giving you that loan. If you hadn't turned things around and paid her back, she would have gone bankrupt too."

Mark sat silently in disbelief. Tears began to stream down his face. "Thanks for telling me, Mom." He sucked in a deep breath. "I have to go. Love you."

"Love you too, son," she said, sad at the pain etched all over her son's face. She wanted to hug him to make him feel better, like when he broke his arm all those years ago. Instead, she grinned and added, "Say hi to everyone for me."

He nodded and quickly hung up, not wanting his mother to see him cry any further.

Dale J. Moore

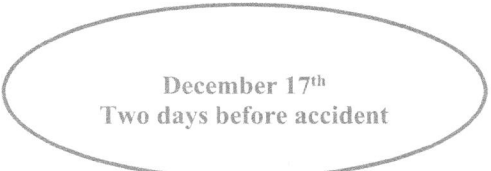

8 *The Weekly Calls - Heather*

Lizzie Montgomery's final call was to her youngest, Heather. Living in a small town in British Columbia was a seismic shift for her daughter. Heather had somewhat resented the move when it happened, but now firmly embraced her lifestyle change. She'd always been keenly aware of environmental issues. Moving to a coastal B.C. town made Heather appreciate nature in a more personal and much more profound way than would have been possible in Toronto.

"Hi, Mom. It's me, the baby of the family!" Heather cheerfully sang through the video screen.

"Hello, dear. Someone's in a good mood today." Lizzie beamed back at her daughter's infectious smile.

"Today's the local Santa Claus parade. You know I've always loved those parades."

"Oh, do I! You'd mark it on the fridge calendar as soon as the date was announced each fall."

"Well, Windsor's parade is huge compared to the one here, but ours is no less festive. Plus now *I* get to toss out the candy from a float."

"I used to laugh at you kids scrambling to pick up the candies off the road."

"Those were the days," Heather laughed. "And the swaps afterward. Mark never liked candy canes. He'd swap me two of those for one rocket. I think I ate candy canes through February!"

"I remember the candy canes disappearing off our tree every year, too."

"Guilty as charged," her daughter grinned.

"So, what's on your float this year? Doing the Christmas tree stand again?"

"Nope. Three years of pine tree pricks and stumbling over fallen pinecones is enough for me. Not to mention the needles all over my clothes."

Mrs. Montgomery laughed. "I think the fake needles are worse nowadays. The vacuum won't even pick them up, no matter how many times I run the beater bar across the floor. I think Maura found errant needles in June last year. There were so many that I really don't know how the tree isn't bare!"

"I remember the fake needles. We bring a small potted tree into the house to decorate. At the end of the season, we take it back outside for Barry to replant in the spring. Less of an environmental impact."

"I've had that artificial tree for over twenty years," her mother replied. "I guess I'm doing my part by not buying a new one."

"That you are," Heather responded with a gleam. "About the parade..." She paused to take a swig of water from her glass. "This year we are doing a *Home Alone* theme. Like the movies. Your grandson is playing Kevin. The float has a house in the centre, with doorways on all sides. He'll go in and out of the doors, moving around the float to hit the crooks with various things, like frying pans, two-by-fours, irons, etc. Yours truly and Barry are the crooks."

Lizzie Montgomery laughed. She'd met her adoptive grandson Kyle once. She remembered the happy surprise when Heather and Barry called with the news. Knowing Heather couldn't have children of her own, she was especially happy for her daughter, even if she was well past typical parenting age when Kyle came into their lives. "I think Kyle will have no problem with the energy required to play that role, but Barry is too nice to play a bad guy!"

Heather grinned back. "He is a sweetheart most of the time. But there are times I wouldn't mind taking a frying pan to him." She laughed. "No, I'm kidding, of course. We used discarded Styrofoam to make replicas of all the hitting items so nobody gets hurt."

"Sounds like a fun family outing and a great Christmas memory to share."

"Thanks, Mom, I think it will be."

"Make sure you get pictures," her mother replied. She looked at her daughter, happiness beaming from her beautiful face. It warmed her inside to see her youngest so happy. It wasn't always that way, she recalled. After a year at St. Clair college, Heather had left Windsor for Toronto. She soon met a guy who turned into a real scumbag. Jeff regularly hit her. Gone were Heather's skirts and short-sleeve tops, replaced with pants and long sleeves. Anything that could hide the bruises became accessories – along with creative makeup use. The girl that previously never wore sunglasses or head scarves could have become their spokeswoman. Following a few months of abuse, Heather finally thought she'd mustered the courage to leave Jeff. Then she found out she was pregnant. Not wanting to become a single mother, she stayed. Even after she told him and he beat her for getting pregnant, she stayed. Like many men with explosive tempers, Jeff would apologize profusely afterward, saying that it would never happen again. Until the next time.

"Mom? Mom?"

Mrs. Montgomery snapped out of her trance. "Sorry, dear. I was lost in an old memory."

Heather frowned. "I figured as much. The talk of getting hit with a frying pan did it, didn't it?"

Her mother frowned, apologizing. "I'm sorry, dear."

"No, it's okay. I'm over it. Mary convincing me to leave Toronto after Jeff mysteriously moved out was the best advice I ever got. My life here is great. Barry is great. Being a mother to Kyle is amazing," she coughed, "most of the time, anyways." She laughed.

Her mother paused, not knowing if she should come clean. Perhaps enough time had passed. "There's more to that story, dear. I think it's time you heard it."

"Did Dad or one of my brothers scare him off?" She firmly placed her hands on her hips. "I knew one of them must have threatened Jeff. He was too nuts to just leave without striking out one more time, like a parting gift to me."

"Close, but it was your sister Mary who got him to leave."

Heather looked puzzled, leaning back in her chair. "Mary? How …?"

"Well, when you miscarried after one of his beatings, Mary had heard enough."

"But I never told Mary that Jeff beat me."

"Oh, dear." Her mother looked sadly at her. "We both knew. You couldn't fool your mother or sister. Mary took some pictures of your bruising when you were tanning and fell asleep at my place." She watched her daughter take a deep breath. "Mary lured Jeff to lunch on the premise of interviewing him for a character in her new thriller – and a free lunch with drinks."

"He would never turn down free drinks," Heather meekly replied. "Nor know when to stop," she mumbled, unclear if her mother heard.

"Mary picked the outdoor patio of a restaurant across from a Toronto police station. She knew their security cameras recorded everything around the entire building, plus surrounding streets. Mary asked the waitress ahead of time to stall on the meals but keep the drinks coming. Jeff was half in the bag when Mary confronted him about abusing you. He of course denied it, but she kept pushing him, taunting him. She later said she couldn't remember what exactly pushed him over the line. She assumed it was one of two lines. It was either calling him a 'spineless little man' or saying that 'guys with tiny dicks hit women', pardon my language."

Heather laughed, not used to hearing language like that from her mother. "Either would have done it," she replied.

Her mother continued. "Jeff started by getting loud, then began screaming. He totally lost it. He started to wail on your sister with his fists. A few nearby male patrons jumped in to subdue him. He took a few good punches in the melee. Mary said she thought the one guy was going to beat him to death, but the other guys got him to stop." She stopped to look for a reaction from her daughter. Heather's face had paled. "Mary told me the police were there in minutes. Mary received medical treatment for her cuts and bruises then she gave her statement to the police. She also produced the tanning pictures of your battered body. She asked if an immediate restraining order could get issued. The order was ready prior to Jeff's release on bail. He had two days to move out of your apartment. He did so under the supervision of police officers the next day."

Heather looked stunned, her earlier glow replaced by a ghostly complexion. "I came home to find his key left with the super. No explanation. No note. Nothing."

"It wasn't a coincidence Mary showed up the day he moved out. She also knew the restraining order might get overturned by Jeff's lawyer at any time. That's why she was so pushy to get you to move out. She was worried he'd come back to take it out on you again."

"She was emphatic that I move out immediately," Heather recalled. "I couldn't say no to her. She knew that. We all looked up to Mary. We knew she had a special gift for managing and fixing problems. I didn't realize how far she went to help me out."

"That was our Mary," her mother beamed.

Heather used a knuckle to wipe away a small tear, then suddenly burst out laughing.

"What's so funny, dear?"

"I just remembered when I opened the door for her that day. She had sunglasses and a head scarf wrapped around her face. I made a joke about her mimicking my style." She paused. "I didn't realize until now that it was for the same reason I had that style – to hide the bruising from that jerk." She sighed. "I didn't realize at the time that I used the disguise to save my pride too."

Dale J. Moore

December 22nd
Morning

9   Maura Visits The Hospital

Maura's restless night wreaked havoc on her stomach this morning, three days before Christmas Day. Receiving a call late yesterday afternoon informing her that Lizzie was moving out of isolation had eased her anxiety down a notch from the extremely high level she'd suffered since the accident. Those few days felt like the longest of her life. At this moment, the idea of sitting at Lizzie's bedside seemed worse than watching her late mother in her final days. Her mother's demise came quickly following a surprise heart attack. This – this problem – she had caused by her inaction. She didn't know how to deal with the guilt, despite Dr. Raymond stating it wasn't her fault.

Maura thought about the phone calls she'd made after the accident. One to each of Lizzie's children. She had thought of emailing them to save herself some agony, but she knew that wasn't the right thing to do. Dr. Raymond had made a point of the importance of persuading the children to come to their mother's bedside. An email couldn't articulate the direness in the same way as a direct conversation. She recalled the calls she'd made, starting with Heather, who'd acted the most pleasant. Heather wanted to jump on a plane to get there immediately, but agreed there was no point until her mother came out of isolation. A second call that night detailed her arrival time late today. Maura wished all the calls had gone that way.

The oldest son Kevin had talked kindly on the first call. He must have thought about the incident in the days between, because last night he expressed agitation about having to leave at Christmas. He'd also questioned why Maura had let it happen. He wasn't happy, but apologized after her explanation, knowing how stubborn his mother could be. He'd fly in from Nova Scotia today, on the same connector from Toronto as Heather, if nothing delayed their first flights.

When it came to the other sons, it was a very different story. The first call to each of them resulted in Maura breaking down in tears. They were both very rough on her. They practically screamed at her for letting it happen. Perhaps their businessmen backgrounds led to high expectations of the 'hired help'. Perhaps they were both just total jerks who treated employees like crap. She didn't know any of the boys, really. She'd overheard them on a few Sunday calls, that was it. None of them had visited in the five years of her employment with their mother. Prior to Maura's hiring, Heather had visited one summer with her husband and son. They were on their way to Toronto to visit Ron, taking a cross country road trip. Heather confessed to Maura during the day's earlier phone call that they really wanted their son to see Toronto, and Ron's place was cheaper than a hotel. It was Heather who'd convinced her mother to find a live-in assistant to lend a hand. Maura interviewed and got the job.

After parking and locking her car, Maura tentatively walked toward the hospital. Did she purposely park in the cheap lot, so she'd have a longer walk to delay the inevitable? Maybe, she thought. She stopped inside the hospital to pick up a tall coffee for herself. She hoped she could withstand a long visit without breaking down into a blubbering mess. Asking directions at the nurses' station on the floor, she proceeded down the hall. She slowly entered the room, almost creeping as she proceeded, unsure of what lay ahead. Fear gripped her body, stiffening her legs to the point of causing pain in each small step.

Maura had researched burn victims on the internet, trying to understand the healing process and get some visuals of what to expect. The harsh reality of seeing her boss, and friend, covered in bandages shocked her system. She gasped for breaths, almost dropping her coffee at the sight. She fell heavily into the visitor's chair and wept. A nurse entered the room to comfort Maura, handing her Kleenex until she'd calmed down. Once the nurse left, Maura removed her heavy coat, draping it over her chair. Settled down, she started talking to Lizzie, first in fractured sentences about the weather, then finally full sentences about her calls to Lizzie's children. The good and the bad, and the true hope that they all made the effort to come. Through it all, Lizzie slept. Whether she heard or comprehended anything, Maura couldn't tell but the doctor had told her to talk to her friend. She did, hoping that subconsciously some part was getting through.

Sitting at Lizzie's bedside, her stomach finally felt settled enough to eat a home-made bifanna sandwich. Deep in thought about her friend as she nibbled, the vibrations of her phone on the nearby table startled her. She placed her sandwich down to read the text. It was the flight number and time for Mark's arrival from Calgary tomorrow. Hopefully he was more pleasant in person. He had to be. She had no idea when Ron was coming. He said he'd drive. That was all she knew. She didn't press him for details, just wanting the call to end.

Closing her eyes to savour the last bite of her sandwich, she collected her thoughts. No more stalling. She took a drink of cold coffee and cleared her throat.

"Mrs. Montgomery," she started formally. "It is my sad duty to tell you that I am resigning from your employment, effective in two weeks. I have failed in my duties and must pay the consequences. I have prepared a resignation letter" — she paused to hold the letter up to the sleeping woman, — "and I will give it to Heather when she arrives tonight. I want to say thank you for the trust that you've had in me, and for the dear friendship we've developed." She stopped, tears flowing freely, her hands shaking the letter she held out. "But your trust was mislaid. I will never be able to tell you how sorry I am for letting this happen to you." She choked on the last few words, not sure if they left her mouth or she'd just tried to say them and failed. She looked at Lizzie, as if expecting a response. She neatly folded up the resignation letter back into the envelope labeled 'Heather'. Maura stood up to put on her coat. She looked at her friend one more time, then leaned over to kiss her gently on her bandaged forehead, hoping not to cause her any more pain.

December 22nd
Afternoon

10   The First Arrivals

Approaching Vancouver in the air at the end of her two-hour flight from Prince Rupert, Heather thought back to her first trip to the area. She didn't technically make it to the City of Glass. Or 'the Couve' as some called it. She'd made the trip to Vancouver Island from up north in an old beater van with eight friends. It was a combination of driving and ferry ride. Truth be told, the van likely wouldn't have made it if they had to drive the whole way. They were idealistic twenty-somethings, determined to make a difference by marching in a Clayoquot Sound protest on Vancouver Island. It was the nineties, not the sixties, but they channeled their inner hippies both in attire and attitude. Heather's hair was long, wavy, and completely brown back then, long since changed to display natural streaks of grey. She was single and enjoying her independence, though she had a small crush on one of the guys travelling with her. What was his name? She closed her eyes, trying to conjure a mental image. Dan? Don? Maybe. It didn't matter. He'd long since moved away from Prince Rupert. The group had a simple common belief – nature and its creatures needed protection from human interference, whether that meant hunting, destruction of habitat, or pollution. Logging pristine lands fell squarely in that belief. They'd made signs at home to voice their opinions. They were ready to scream as loud as they could when they arrived at the protest. The march got off to a peaceful start. Even the drizzly rain couldn't put a damper on Heather's spirit, and her feeling that she was making a difference. They'd formed a human chain to block the arrival of logging company vehicles. It worked. Unfortunately, the guy she had a crush on decided to throw a rock at one of the logging company workers. A small melee ensued, resulting in Heather getting arrested for disturbing the peace, despite curling up in a ball behind her sign, afraid of the chaos that reigned around her. Others in her group wore the arrest as a badge of honour. Heather felt more embarrassed than righteous. When, ultimately, the protests were successful and laws changed, the embarrassment faded. She felt pride in her part in causing change. When her group sought other environmental causes to protest, Heather decided one arrest was enough. She was done with mass protests, and her crush on the rock thrower. She turned her attention to what good she could personally do in her life and local community.

She drifted off to a sound sleep shortly after takeoff from Vancouver on her way to Toronto. Finding the Windsor departure gate upon arrival, Heather had warmly greeted her brother Kevin after his flight from Halifax. It was a short reunion considering the long absence. Boarding for their Windsor connection was soon announced. They'd agreed to split a cab to their mother's home, where they would use her cars. They assumed Ron would drive from Toronto. They joked about his love for cars, wondering what shiny new toy he'd show up driving this time.

Maura answered the musical doorbell, after a quick check of the peephole to see the delivery guy holding a package, looking down at his phone. She'd expected the last Christmas delivery for the past few days and was happy it had finally arrived. She opened the door, shocked to see the hat of the delivery guy lift to reveal the vile Danny Miller. She tried to slam the door shut, but he stuck a foot in the door, then dropped the package to firmly plant his hand on the door.

Danny looked at Maura, then the package. "Oops, I hope it wasn't anything breakable."

"What do you want?" Maura barked at him. She staggered a few short steps back to temporary safety.

"I'm here for my Christmas bonus, or should I say bonuses," he grinned, eying her up and down.

"You said tomorrow," Maura replied.

"Yeah, I thought I'd come early. Surely the old dame has sent you to the bank by now."

"Well, she hasn't. And she won't have it tomorrow, either," she replied defiantly.

"And why not?" Danny sucked in part of his oversized gut, trying to look intimidating.

"She's in the hospital, you jerk," she responded. "She's likely going to be in there for weeks if not months."

His stare felt like it penetrated her clothing. She crossed her arms in front of her chest, aware of his leering and possible intentions. She looked around the foyer for something to use to defend herself.

"Sounds serious," he said quietly. "I may have to take payment in some other form for now." He took a step forward. "I think a little Mexican might be satisfying."

She took a step backward, defensively latching onto the mop behind her. He stopped suddenly. Then she heard why. A car had pulled up in the driveway.

Danny quickly backed off to stand in the doorway outside the house.

"Well, look the hell who's here!" he exclaimed.

Heather paid the driver while Kevin unloaded their suitcases. She took her bag from her brother then turned to face the house she hadn't seen in a couple of years. The house still loomed large compared to the houses in her town in B.C. She studied the brick structure. It was beautiful, but it wasn't home. Home had sold not too long after their father had passed away. She remembered telling her mother to get a smaller home that she could maintain, knowing a condo without a large yard was out of the question. There were plenty of homes in the Windsor area that had large yards but weren't close to the six thousand square feet of finished living space of this one. Kevin had agreed at the time. Real Estate Ron, however, convinced their mother that a new home this size could easily triple in value before she'd need to move into a nursing home, while the smaller houses would only increase a bit. Location, location, location. Coincidentally, the house was the last house completed by her late father's construction company prior to its sale. Ground was broken the day before her father passed. The family had an option to buy the house during the company sale since it hadn't sold up front. Somehow, knowing that her father had broken ground on the house made from his plans made the place feel a bit more like their home.

As the Montgomery children each wheeled their own bag toward the porch, Danny called out to Kevin.

"Hey, how's the old wide receiver doing?" Three years Kevin's senior, Danny was his quarterback for a single season in school. "You still look like you could run a post route, buddy."

Kevin tried a grin. He was used to Danny's bull. "You got the old part right. My knees would likely give out ten yards into the route." He looked at Danny. "You look like you're cramming for a lineman role."

Danny sneered at him, attempting to suck in his overflowing gut. "Nothing but muscle." He slapped his stomach, which humourously jiggled. "I'm as fit as a nineteen-year-old, pal," he replied with a tinge of hostility.

Heather quickly covered her mouth to avoid laughing out loud. "Excuse me," she said to Danny, walking past with her bag to greet Maura. She then turned to Danny. "Nice suit, by the way. Was that one of your dad's? It looks familiar." She winked at Maura.

Danny grunted a 'humph' sound. "No chance. My suits are all custom-made. They aren't cheap off-the-rack rags."

Kevin approached, giving the suit a once-over. "Nice lines," he sarcastically commented, looking at one leg with a straight pinstripe and the other leg's lines crossing his leg. It also looked like Danny's tailor had used old cloth that he couldn't get rid of. "It's a beaut, Clark."

Heather couldn't help herself this time and laughed out loud at the *Christmas Vacation* reference.

Danny didn't get the joke. "Thanks, Kev, man."

"You still working at your dad's car lot?" Kevin inquired.

"No sir. The old man passed away about seven years ago. The place is all mine now," he proclaimed, puffing out his chest.

"I'm sorry about your loss," Kevin replied.

Danny looked confused. "Loss? I got the car lot."

"I meant your father." Kevin looked incredulously at him.

Danny shrugged his shoulders, making a 'so what' face. "No great loss. The old man never listened to my business ideas. I'm glad he's out of my way."

"I think he valued your partnership," Kevin replied. "After all, he changed the name to Millers Motors."

"So what? That was his name."

"You don't get it. It was Miller's Motors, with an apostrophe. He changed it to Millers Motors plural, because multiple Millers ran it."

Danny looked at him, puzzled. "Nah, you're wrong." Like spotting a shiny object, another thought made its way to his brain. "Why don't you stop by the dealership? We can get caught up. I've got a nice bottle of scotch in my desk."

"I don't drink anymore," Kevin replied.

Danny stared at him, then laughed. "Whatever. You guys should stop by. I'll show you how I've improved the place. I'm open today and tomorrow until nine. Christmas Eve until five."

Kevin forced a smile, thinking a visit with Danny was the last thing he wanted to do while back in the Windsor area. "Sure, we'll see if we can fit it in, right, sis?"

Heather was talking to Maura and not really paying attention. "Sure, sounds good," she replied, deaf to the conversation and hoping she wouldn't regret it later.

"Awesome," Danny stated, shaking Kevin's hand. He leaned back toward the door opening and looked at Maura. "I'll come back tomorrow to pick that item up. Unless you prefer my other offer." He flashed a wicked, toothy grin, then left with his usual swagger.

Kevin pulled his bag into the foyer, closing the door behind him. Maura moved past him, turning the deadbolt lock. Kevin looked at Heather, wondering what they'd missed that compelled Maura to lock the door.

"I'll tell you later," Maura told them, seeing their uncomfortable gazes. "I need to calm down a bit."

Heather gave a sympathetic look to her mother's house aide. "I'm sorry. Danny can be a real jerk." She leaned forward, hugging Maura. Heather stepped back, her hands still softly on Maura's shoulders. "When you're ready, I'm here." She glanced at Kevin. "We'll do what we can to help. Okay?" she added in a soothing voice.

Maura nodded, whispering a thank you.

Kevin looked regretfully at Maura. "I want to apologize for my outburst the other day. It was wrong, unkind, and not like me at all. I think I was in shock, not that that's an excuse for my behaviour."

"Thank you. It was nothing," Maura replied, shrugging. "Nothing compared to your brothers, I can tell you that." A weak smile crossed her face.

"Don't worry about them," Heather assured her. "They'll warm up to you. They like to act tough, but they are softies at heart." She looked at Kevin who didn't seem as sure as her. "Except maybe to each other at times."

Maura nodded politely. "I'm truly sorry for what happened to your mother."

The statement brought them all back to the moment. An awkward minute of silence followed.

Heather coughed and collected her thoughts. "Is that your room, Maura?" she asked. On the right was a small bedroom, replacing the den Sharon had redecorated all those years ago.

"Yes, it is. There is another bedroom down the hall; opposite the guest bathroom and before the master bedroom at the end."

"Oh, we won't use the bedroom on this floor," Heather quickly replied.

"It's a nice room and never gets used," Maura offered. "Though your mother doesn't let me dust in there, so I'd need a few minutes to get it ready."

"That was Mary's room," Heather answered, a slight quiver in her voice. "At the end, when she had to move home."

"Oh, I'm sorry. Of course."

Kevin nodded, tilting his head at the angled wooden staircase.

"We'll just head upstairs to grab a couple of rooms."

"You must be hungry," Maura stated. "Do you want me to heat up some leftover pasta?"

"As good as I'm sure that is, we're both dying for a Windsor style pizza. Can you do us a favour and order a large pizza? What do you want on it, Kev?"

"Mushrooms, pepperoni, green peppers, and bacon. Sound good?"

Heather nodded. "Oh, and if they ask, canned mushrooms, not fresh. It's a Windsor thing."

Lizzie's children claimed rooms for their stay. They cleaned up in time for the arrival of the pizza. As they sat around the kitchen table devouring the style of pizza they'd missed over the years, Heather asked how her mother was doing. She and Kevin had decided to wait until the next day to visit, having endured a long day of flights and layovers.

"The doctor says she's doing good. Especially good for a woman of her age."

"That's encouraging," Heather replied between bites. "How does she look?"

Maura sighed. "You can't tell. She looks like a mummy. Her entire head is bandaged, aside from her mouth and eyes. Even most of her nose and ears are covered. I talked to her for hours, but I don't think she heard me."

"Talking is good, I hear. I think hearing familiar voices is supposed to help." Heather gently laid her hand on top of Maura's.

She could see Kevin looking a little agitated; she motioned to him to hold his tongue.

Maura reached into her pocket, pulling out the resignation letter. She slid it toward Heather. "Here is my two weeks' notice. Please accept it on your mother's behalf."

"Oh, Maura," Heather sighed.

Kevin reached across and grabbed it. Heather quickly put her hand on his before he could open it.

"We'll look at it tomorrow, okay?" Heather told her. "I think we all just need to relax tonight. It's been a long day for all of us."

December 23rd
Late Morning

11   The Second Arrivals

Following a leisurely breakfast two days before Christmas, Kevin and Heather dressed and sought to prepare themselves mentally for their hospital visit. Kevin dreaded the trip. He always took bad news very hard. His ability to process sad news without breaking down got worse as he aged. His wife teased him about crying during sad scenes in movies to the point he wouldn't go to the theatre anymore. He'd thought a *Star Wars* flick would be safe, but he bawled his eyes out when his favourite character died. That was the last movie he saw at a theatre.

When Mary's illness progressed to the point of terminal, Kevin was a complete mess. Being the closest in age to their oldest sibling made it particularly hard on him. On top of the devastating loss was that awful feeling of mortality. Though he felt Heather had a closer bond to Mary after Heather reached her late teens, he felt he owned that tie with Mary through their teens and into their twenties. Whether it was his bond with Mary in their formative years, or her help to get his life back on track, he knew he owed her a debt he could never repay. Now, he wondered for the first time, how could he ever pay his mother back for everything she had done? The thought choked him up to the point that he gagged and coughed as he heard Heather ask him something.

"I'm sorry, Heather," he coughed again. "What did you ask?"

"I asked if you wanted me to drive, but I'll take your visit to la-la land as a yes, I should drive." She snatched the keys to her mother's Jeep from the table in the foyer. "You okay, Kev?" she asked as they entered the garage from the house.

"Yeah, fine," he lied as they passed the blue BMW sports car on their way to the Jeep. "You know me. I'm sure I'll be present when we see her."

Kevin remained quiet, not even remarking as Heather stopped backing out of the garage, afraid she was about to separate the side mirror from the Jeep. She glanced at her brother, who said nothing as she pulled ahead, turned the wheel, and tried again to navigate a damage-free exit from the garage. As she turned the car to pull out of the driveway, the passenger front wheel dropped onto the ground with a thud. She jerked the wheel and straightened out the Jeep. Again, Kevin didn't flinch.

Heather slowly steered the car through the quiet neighbourhood, wanting to look over the mini mansions on both sides, but more concerned about scraping the few visiting vehicles on the road. She jumped in her seat when her brother spoke.

"You do still have your licence, don't you?"

"Of course I do," she answered, somewhat miffed.

"It doesn't show," Kevin squawked back. He closed one eye as she turned left, narrowly missing the car at the corner. "When was the last time you drove a car?"

"It's not a car, it's a Jeep. It's a little bigger than I'm used to."

"What do you drive now?" he inquired.

"We have an F-150 pickup," she proudly replied.

"And you find a Jeep big compared to it?" he asked, puzzled.

"I said we have an F-150, not that I drive it."

"So, what do you drive?"

She blushed. "I don't. Barry drives. Or I walk. It's a small community."

Kevin took a deep breath and exhaled. "Maybe I should drive. I'm not sure you can park this thing when we get there." He paused a second. "If we get there."

"Hey, I haven't hit anything!" she protested. "Yet," she added.

"You barely escaped the garage. Technically, yes, when you drove on the lawn you didn't hit anything."

She blushed again. "I thought you were zoned out back there."

"I wish I was."

She checked her mirrors, then pulled over. "You're right," she grinned as she released her seat belt. "I don't think I can get this thing into a parking spot."

Kevin parked in the closest lot he could find and pressed the auto-lock on the Jeep's key fob. Finding a Tim's inside the hospital, Heather had the staff put her coffee in a thermal mug she'd brought from her mother's home. Kevin ordered a bottle of water for the hospital room. On their mother's floor, Heather approached the nurses' station.

"Excuse me, please?" she asked demurely.

"Yes, how can I help you?" came the response.

"Could I get a box of tissues for my mother's room?"

"What room?" the nurse asked.

"707. Mrs. Montgomery"

The nurse looked at her, puzzled. "Is she your mother?"

"Yes. She is our mother."

"You know that she is not responsive. She'll have no need for additional tissues."

Heather smiled and leaned forward. "We are aware. They aren't for her; they are for us." In front of her body, she pointed back toward her brother.

The nurse looked at Kevin's slightly swollen eyes and nodded. "Sure." She pushed her chair back to look under the counter. "Here. Let me know if you need anything else."

"Thank you," Heather replied, then whispered one more comment. "I'll let you know if he passes out."

The nurse looked at Kevin, grinned, then turned her attention back to her reports.

As they walked away, Kevin asked what that was about.

"Oh, nothing. Girl stuff."

"Did you tell her the whole box was for me, or something to that effect?"

"No." She put on her poker face. "If you must know, she asked if you were single. I told her no."

"Yeah, I'm sure that's what she asked."

Heather laughed, then pointed. "Mom's room is the next one on the left."

As she crossed the threshold of the room, Heather stopped in her tracks, causing Kevin to bump into her. He looked up to see the problem. A man with jet black hair in a long black trench coat stood beside the bed.

"Ron? Is that you?" Heather asked.

Ron turned. "Hey, little sis." He tried to smile, but he'd obviously been crying. "And you brought Kev with you too!"

They exchanged brief hugs before Ron stepped aside to reveal the state of their mother to the others.

Heather gasped, both hands quickly covering her mouth, the box of tissues tumbling to the floor. Ron leaned hard on the end of the bed, like a novice sailor trying to find his sea legs.

"Oh my," Heather uttered.

"Yeah," Ron replied. "It's hard to imagine that Mom's in there," he motioned around with his hand, "under all those bandages."

Kevin gingerly bent over to recover the box of tissues, yanking a couple quickly toward his nose.

"I'm glad you brought some more," Ron smiled. He pointed to the garbage can in the corner. "I've almost cleaned out the other box."

"At least she looks like she's not in pain," Heather commented.

"I'm sure she's loaded up with morphine." Ron looked at her intravenous tube. "Likely in her drip."

Kevin stared at his mother. "It's hard to tell it's her," he sniffled. "Her head is completely covered and both hands are bandaged."

Heather looked around. "I'll ask Maura to bring up some of Mom's things, like maybe the five-by-seven picture of Mom and Dad from the living room."

"I checked the chart earlier," Ron offered. "I wanted to make sure I wasn't blubbering over a complete stranger," he laughed.

"That would be embarrassing if some other family came in, wondering why you were weeping for their mother."

Ron laughed back. "That would happen to Mark, not me. He's the one that usually charges ahead without looking." He paused to look at his watch. "When is he getting here by the way?"

"Last we knew, late this afternoon," Kevin answered.

"How long have you been here?" Heather asked Ron.

"Maybe an hour."

"And you drove this morning?" Kevin questioned.

"Yeah, after my workout. Showered and hopped in the car, hair still wet."

"What time did you get up?" Heather wondered.

"Five-thirty. Same as every day," Ron grinned.

"Do yourself a favour," Heather said, "and don't get me up tomorrow morning at that time, unless of course you want a beating with a frying pan."

Ron laughed. "I guess that's two-thirty your time. Have you adjusted yet?"

"It's the first day, so no," she grumbled.

Kevin had ignored much of the banter, his hand on the bed beside his mother. "I think Maura said we're supposed to talk to Mom, even though she likely can't hear us."

"That's what the doctors suggest. Do you want to go first, since you're the oldest?" Heather caught herself. "The oldest now."

"Agreed," Ron replied. "Let me grab another chair so all of us can sit. It's going to be a long morning."

As the clock rolled toward twelve-thirty, Heather finished catching her mother up on the latest with the Christmas parade, as well as other goings-on with her family and community. During the past two hours, Elizabeth Montgomery's children had found out more about each other's current lives than they had in the past ten years. They all enjoyed hearing about each other. Ron even kept his boasting to a minimum. Kevin did the same with his sobbing.

They took turns saying goodbye to their mother, promising to come back the next day, Christmas Eve. They told her Maura would visit for a few hours late in the afternoon. Heather thought her mother's hand twitched at the mention of Maura. She shook it off as imagined.

Dale J. Moore

December 23rd
Afternoon

12   The Grudge

Driving his new blue metallic Cadillac CTV-5 Blackwing from Toronto
had felt like pure bliss for Ron. He'd only taken delivery a couple of
months earlier and had barely left the confines of downtown Toronto
driving it. They had closed the cottage by the time he got the car. A
good run to Muskoka would have to wait for spring. It felt great cutting
loose this morning between London and Windsor. Having that monster
engine at his command energized his soul.

Driving from the hospital back to his mother's home, he
reflected on his thoughts during his morning drive. He'd told himself to
'play nice' with Mark when the two met, likely later today. They'd had
a history of run-ins over the years, sometimes barely able to stay in the
same room as one another. Mark blamed Ron, and Ron blamed Mark.
Deep down, Ron knew he was the one to blame. Always had been, ever
since Mark changed from the gangly teenager that Ron could tease and
push around, to the young man that suddenly became faster, stronger,
and dare he say, better looking than him. Ron self-described as uber-
competitive. He despised losing. It was a terrible feeling to have his
four-year-younger sibling suddenly run and skate faster than him. He
didn't like it one bit. He could live with Kevin occasionally skating

faster, since he was older, stronger. But his little brother? That was grating.

Having put up with years of teasing and brotherly bullying, Mark started to push back. One day at the rink, during a pickup game with the neighbourhood guys, Mark skated back into his end of the ice to retrieve an errant pass. Ron chased him down. As Mark turned to go around the net, Ron leapt off his skates and drilled Mark heavily into the boards. He knew he'd hit his younger brother good, taking the puck and circling the net. When he turned to shoot at the net, he saw the back of the goalie looking at Mark writhing in pain on the ice. He'd separated Mark's shoulder with the hit – though Mom always said he'd broken his arm. Ron felt little remorse at the time, saying Mark should have seen the hit coming and prepared for it. Nobody else on the ice saw it that way.

The rift grew wider with the passing of years. He remembered a blowup one Christmas when he accused Mark of cheating at a game of Rail Baron. Kevin sided with Mark, making Ron more furious, especially since they were right. Mark had beaten them fair and square. Ron had gravitated to a place where he couldn't stand losing anything to his baby brother. Ron avoided Mark for the rest of the holiday, aside from Christmas dinner. His mother was not pleased in the least at his childish behaviour and let him know.

The final straw in their fragile relationship came when Mark got bailed out of financial problems by their father. Ron received no assistance despite almost begging. His dad had told him he didn't lend money to family, yet turned around and did exactly that for Mark. Though it made sense for Ron to feel angry with his father and not with

Mark, it was easier to blame Mark. It was years before Ron found out that Mary had engineered the loan to Mark. Leave it to her to convince their father to break his rule. Ron couldn't hold anything against Mary. How could anyone? She'd done so much for everyone, including helping Ron manage his competitiveness and understanding boundaries when engaging in 'friendly competition'. By the time he found out that Mary had been involved in the loan, he'd driven a wedge so far between him and his brother, he doubted it could ever be removed. He chose to take the road of pretending that none of it ever happened. He didn't know if he had it in him to apologize. And it would take a lot of apologizing. Maybe, though, it was time. Fences don't mend themselves.

Dale J. Moore

December 23rd
Afternoon

13   Confession

Maura met Ron when the Montgomery children returned from the hospital. Like Kevin, Ron apologized for his outburst on the phone. Maura made sandwiches, deferring another request for pizza. She sat with them to eat, happy they were so welcoming in person, as opposed to over the phone. Heather filled Maura in on their mother's condition, including that she thought her mother's finger twitched. They asked Maura to recount the accident now that she'd had time to reflect. Maura walked through the minutes prior to the accident, describing what she saw happen. It brought her to tears, again – a regular occurrence this past week. She felt relief that Lizzie's children all expressed how she'd done nothing wrong. They knew if their strong-willed mother decided she was going to do something, it would take an act of nature or God to stop her.

"Thank you for your kindness," Maura said, wiping at the continued stream of tears. "It means a lot to me. I will try not to feel too guilty."

Heather reached out to Maura's hand resting on the table, patting it reassuringly.

Maura looked up from her tears, directly at Heather. "I should tell you about yesterday and that creep Mr. Miller."

"Just call him Danny," Kevin replied. "He doesn't deserve the respect that comes with saying Mister."

"I'll keep saying Mr. Miller, if that's okay," Maura said. "First names are for friends."

"Fair enough," Kevin conceded.

"Well, Mr. Miller has gotten more suggestive every month when he comes to visit."

"He comes by every month?" Ron asked, puzzled as to why.

"Yes, he gets his money from your mother. Something about a promise your father made."

The siblings waited for her continue, unaware of any promise. Maura sat quietly, her head staring into her lap. She looked afraid to speak.

"What did Mr. Miller do?" Heather gently asked as she leaned forward to offer comfort.

Maura looked up briefly. She returned to looking down, mumbling, and nervously rubbing the silver cross hanging around her neck.

"It's okay, Maura," Heather consoled her. "What did Mr. Miller do to you?"

"I think yesterday he was about to rape me." She sheepishly looked at Heather, avoiding eye contact with Kevin, "but you showed up and he quickly backed off."

"Did he touch you?" Heather asked, startled by the conversation.

"Not this time. Last time when your mother was here, yes. She told him she was ending the payments, that your father never meant to pay him indefinitely. Danny had threatened lawsuits over Christopher's death and his accident cutting down the tree. Your father didn't think Danny had a legal leg to stand on, but didn't want the family or his company dragged through the news. Lizzie said she'd continued the payments out of pity, not guilt. Now that he was a successful businessman, he shouldn't need a handout anymore."

"Good for her," Ron stated.

"He then threatened her, asking for more money this week – he called it a Christmas bonus." She looked down at the napkin that she nervously twisted in her hands. "When she said no, he grabbed me around the neck and started thrusting himself at me from behind. He said he'd rape me right there in front of your mother if she didn't agree to pay the bonus."

"I assume that Mom told him she'd pay so he'd let you go," Heather said sadly.

Maura nodded, burying her face in her hands. She broke down in tears again.

Heather stood, moving over to embrace the sitting woman from behind. She handed Maura a box of tissues.

Kevin sat, flabbergasted.

Ron sat, fuming. "We need to get him to stop. We need to get him locked up." He looked at his siblings. "We need a plan."

Dale J. Moore

December 23rd
Afternoon

14   *A Plan*

Heather had helped Maura to her room, giving her a Tylenol to help with the headache brought on by all the tears. Maura also took an anti-nauseant to help her rest. Heather rejoined her brothers at the kitchen table.

"Danny's always been a slimeball," Kevin said.

"He gives us sales guys a bad name," Ron responded.

Kevin raised an eyebrow. "Isn't that the pot calling the kettle black?"

Ron looked insulted. "I may be the king of upsell, but I always sell legitimate products or services." He took a drink of water. "Danny, he's a piece of work, at least from what I've heard from some former classmates over the years."

Kevin grinned. "I don't know how you find the time to stay in touch with everyone."

"It's part of my job. You're only as successful as your network in my business. Contacts lead to sales."

"I'll take your word for it," Kevin replied. "What have your contacts had to say about the scumbag Danny Miller?"

"We all knew Danny's father. He was a good businessman. Honest. Trustworthy. Danny is nothing like that. Danny is the king of the scheme. He's got more cons going on in that dealership than I've got fingers."

"Such as?" Heather joined the conversation, sitting down with an herbal tea.

"First, the simple ones. Rolling back odometers. Painting tires to make them look new. Claiming to install new parts without doing it."

Kevin shook his head.

Ron continued. "He'll also show used cars with nice seat covers that conceal torn cushions and stains then deliver them without the covers. If someone complains after the sale, he doesn't recall that the car ever had seat covers but he happens to have some available for sale."

"That's horrible," Heather grumbled.

"He does the same with floor mats and sometimes even with tires. Customers are too excited when they pick up the car to notice the bait and switches. His contracts all state something like 'as delivered' in fine print. As soon as the customer signs and takes the keys, they are committed, usually without rechecking the car until they get in to drive it away."

"How does he get away with that? Isn't it illegal?" Kevin questioned. "It sounds illegal to me."

Ron shrugged. "The fine print covers his bases. Of course, there are certain protections offered by the government. Most people don't realize those protections exist or let them lapse fighting with the dealership."

"So how do we get him to back off from Mom?" Kevin asked, clearly frustrated. "I mean, we could wait for Mark to get here then the three of us go intimidate him with bodily harm."

Ron shook his head. "He'd end up threatening us with lawsuits then start bleeding us dry too."

Heather sighed. "There's got to be something."

"We could get him on fraud for turning odometers back. We would need a contract with the stated kilometers. I have a friend at the Ministry of Transportation that can provide the last reported mileage from insurance companies."

"Sounds like a longshot," Kevin moaned.

"Agreed. We'd have to go to the police with proof. Even then, it would take time." Ron shifted in his chair.

"Any other ideas?" Heather asked.

"The only other thing that comes to mind is looking at the agreements he offers for full car maintenance coverage. You know, where you pay a monthly fee, and they supposedly will repair anything and everything that goes wrong with your car. He just got into that business recently, per my source. I doubt they are on the up-and-up. I'd need to see one to confirm."

Heather nodded. "Sure, I've seen commercials for those. I thought those were only in the U.S. though, not Canada."

"We have lots of them in Canada," Ron replied. "Some of the big banks have even moved into that territory. I'm not sure what regulations are in place yet. I'm sure a snake like Danny will skirt them as much as possible. Or just ignore them."

Kevin ran his fingers through his salt-and-pepper hair in frustration. Unconsciously, he began pulling on his greying beard as he thought. "I'm leaning toward the beating. Surely, we can lure him to some remote place without cameras and pound the crap out of him. It will be his word versus ours."

"Mom always told us violence never solved anything," Heather pointed out.

"Yeah, well Mom never played hockey," Ron grinned. "But point taken." He looked at his brother. "We can't resort to violence, as appetizing as it sounds to punch Danny Miller in that smarmy face of his."

"Okay," Kevin agreed. "Then let me go down there to pretend to buy a car with all the upsells. I'll bring the contract back for you to look over and find something we can use."

Heather spoke up. "No, you can't do it. I propose I do it. He thinks all women are stupid sex toys, so he won't suspect my motives."

"I think creepy Danny is into younger women," Ron stated. "No offence meant," he added.

She laughed, tossing back her grey hair. "Some people don't appreciate older women. I'll say we're buying Maura a car on behalf of our mother. A Christmas gift. I suspect just getting him to think about Maura will throw him off his game. When he thinks I'm going to sign the deal, I'll say I must bring the contract home, as Kevin is the power of attorney given Mom's condition. I'll say you'll come back tomorrow, Christmas Eve day, to sign it."

Ron sat up straight, enthused by the plan. "I like it. In the meantime, I'll catch up with my contacts at the police department and the Ministry."

"We have a plan," Kevin smiled. "But if it doesn't work, I'm still thinking of Plan B, as in a beating."

Dale J. Moore

December 23rd
Afternoon

15   *The Last Arrival*

Mark was pleased he'd been able to catch an earlier flight when a spot opened. He'd booked the mid-morning flight but arrived well ahead of the earlier flight and got the first alternate spot on that plane. When a few people cancelled at the last minute, he snapped up a seat, rescheduling the connecting flight to Windsor. With the few hours' change in time zones, it made the difference between arriving late afternoon versus late evening. Thanking and paying the Uber driver, he turned with his suitcase, giving the house a once-over. A builder by trade, he could spot flaws that others, especially over-excited new homeowners, couldn't. His mother's house looked solid. He only spotted one French corner where the mason used a chipped brick. He doubted it occurred post-construction, since it was twelve feet from the ground and not in a place where you'd normally put a ladder. If Dad had lived to oversee the construction, that wouldn't have happened. Just the same, very minor for a house this size. The house was bigger than the homes in the neighbourhood he was currently building, but he'd erected bigger houses in the past.

Mark pressed the doorbell, surprised to hear a musical chime. He tried to place the song. His head hung when he finally recognized the song – "I'll Be Home For Christmas". Wishful thinking on his mother's part, no doubt.

The door opened. Ron stood in the doorway.

"We don't need any!" Ron said, slamming the door in his brother's face.

Mark jumped back, startled.

Ron re-opened the door. "Oh, the look on your face was priceless! I hope Mom's security system recorded that."

"You're still a jerk," Mark rebutted, before stepping forward to shake his brother's hand. Ron shook it uncomfortably. Mark picked up his suitcase. "How long has it been, big brother?"

"Well, since Mary ..." Ron stopped. "Ten years, I guess." He closed the front door. Mark placed his bag on the foyer tile. "And ten pounds, maybe twenty pounds by the look of it," he snipped.

Mark instinctively sucked in his gut. "It's just my success belt. Gives my customers confidence."

"Or makes them feel better about themselves," Ron shot back.

The shots would have gone on, with Mark worrying they'd digress into the inevitable argument. Fortunately, Heather approached them.

"There'll be plenty of time for that later," she laughed, giving Mark a hug.

"You look great," Mark replied.

"Thanks," both Ron and Heather replied.

Ron looked at his brother, shrugging. "Hey, I'm going to take a compliment wherever I can, whether meant for me or not. Especially from you."

Mark shook his head then slipped off his shoes and hung his coat in the foyer closet. "Something smells good," he remarked, nose slightly in the air to enjoy the aroma. "Is that Spago's?" he asked excitedly.

"Spago's is tomorrow," Heather remarked. We ordered it yesterday, fearing they'd be closed Christmas Eve. We'll reheat it tomorrow."

"Oh my god, you read my mind," Mark replied. "I was wondering how I was going to squeeze a meal at Spago's into this trip. I assumed we'd have pizza."

"Last night," Heather replied, leading her brothers toward the kitchen. "We got a king size. There's some left for a snack later."

"So, what is that amazing smell coming from the kitchen?" Mark asked.

"Maura is cooking a traditional Portuguese meal for us. I think she said Porco Preto, which is a pork dish, plus roasted potatoes."

Mark inhaled again. "It smells great."

"Oh, and Caldo Verde – it's a soup, for starters," Heather added.

"Can't wait. I'm starving. When's dinner?" Mark asked.

"Not for a few hours yet," replied Ron. "Once Heather returns."

"Yes," Heather said, moving past Mark to the foyer closet to retrieve her coat. "Best be going." She brushed past him again on her way to the garage. "Wish me luck."

Mark looked perplexed.

"From what Kevin tells me, the other drivers on the road are the ones that need the luck," Ron remarked.

Heather gave Ron a pretend evil glare, sticking her tongue out in the process.

Ron laughed.

She looked back at Mark, a happy glow returning to her face. "I'll explain the car thing later. Can't wait to catch up!"

Ron looked at Mark as the garage entry door closed behind Heather. "Did you want to go see Mom?"

"I was thinking of it, but it's been a long day."

"Nobody will think less of you if you grab a nap," Ron replied. "But then again, when the bar is so low, how could we?"

"Nice …" Mark forced a grin. He shied away from too much banter with Ron – he was so competitive that he always had to get the last shot. "I need a snack though. Any bananas or granola bars in the pantry?"

"You look more like a potato chip kind of guy," Ron teased him.

"Exactly," he laughed, "which is why I'm searching for a healthier option." He touched his smallish but visible gut. He looked around the kitchen, spotting a bowl of bananas. He broke one from the bunch, looking around. "Where's the cook?"

"Not sure," Ron replied. "But I wouldn't try nicking a taste. I think Maura would swat you with a spatula if she caught you."

Mark laughed. "She's learned a few tricks from Mom, I guess." He tossed the banana peel in the garbage. They headed back to the foyer to get his luggage.

"We saved the room at the left upstairs for you."

"Thanks," Mark replied. "By the way, where was Heather off to?"

"She's off to buy a car," Ron stated. "And hopefully catch a crook."

Dale J. Moore

December 23rd
Early Evening

16 Dinner

"Dinner!" yelled Ron upstairs to Mark, as Heather entered the front door. "Maura was starting to worry about you," he told her. "She thought that creep might have done something to you."

Mark lumbered down the stairs, pulling a shirt over his head as he went. He settled the shoulders of the shirt as he reached the landing, where he joined Ron and Heather walking toward the enticing aromas from dinner.

As they entered the kitchen, Kevin turned from in front of the oven, a hot dish prepared by Maura in his hand. "Hey Markie Mark."

"Wow! It's been forever since anybody called me that," Mark laughed.

"It's great to see you, Mark." Kevin replied, placing the hot dish on a serving plate beside a couple of others. He turned to retrieve the last dish, then closed the oven door by flipping it up with his foot then slamming it closed with his hip.

"Still got the moves, I see," laughed Ron.

Maura used a ladle to stir the soup in the large pot on the stove top. She began filling bowls, which Kevin scooped up to carry to the kitchen table, two at a time. Maura pulled off her apron and brought her bowl of soup to the table to join the siblings. Once she sat, the kids all reached for their spoons.

"Hmmm," she cleared her throat.

They stopped to look at her.

"First prayer, then dinner," she stated, bordering on scolding.

"Ah, yes," replied Kevin, spreading his mouth wide to show as many teeth as possible. "The Blessing."

Maura whacked his hand with her spoon.

The other siblings giggled, like they were kids again.

Maura stared at them. They all bowed their heads in compliance.

"Glory be to the Father, and the Son, and the Holy Spirit, now and forever. Through the great deeds of the Lord, we are blessed with this food. Amen."

A round of 'Amens' quietly followed. They looked up to see if it was okay to eat. When Maura dug her spoon into the soup, they followed suit.

"This is incredible," Heather exclaimed. "Is this kale? It seems different."

"Portuguese kale. Similar but better," Maura proudly stated.

"It is awesome," Mark offered. "I'm glad I didn't spoil my appetite when I arrived."

As they neared the end of their soup, the boys got into a slurping contest, circa their early teens. Maura stared bewildered. Heather laughed. Mark was declared winner with the loudest, most disgusting throaty slurp. Even Ron agreed.

"I hope you're not going to do that with the main course," Maura said, having never witnessed such a spectacle at the dinner table.

"Our apologies, Maura." Mark told her. "It's something we did as kids to gross out our mother."

"I'm sure it worked," Maura replied while she gathered the empty bowls and spoons. "I hope there is better conversation around the Porco Preto." She carried the load of dishes toward the sink.

"Speaking of which," Mark turned to Heather. "What's this I hear about you buying Maura a car?"

Bowls and spoons crashed heavily into the sink behind them. They turned to look at Maura, looking like she'd seen a ghost.

"Oh, sorry, Maura," Ron stood up to apologize. "You can breathe again. We're not really buying you a car. It's part of our plan to get rid of Danny Miller."

Maura nodded, the colour returning to her face as she restacked the dishes in the sink.

"So how did it go?" Kevin asked. "I need to know what to expect tomorrow."

"It went much as expected, being the male chauvinist pig that Danny Miller is. It's no wonder he's getting fat. He's so full of himself he needs to expand," she chuckled.

"How do you explain Ron's slim physique then?" laughed Kevin.

"Nice," Ron grinned back.

"Anyway," Heather continued. "I looked up his inventory online yesterday, you know, to get a sense of the prices on his lot. I haven't shopped for a vehicle in forever. Boy, they're expensive now."

She stopped to see heads nodding around the table. "When Danny asked how much I was willing to spend, I had a number ready to give him. I told him about ten grand lower than his top-of-the-line cars and SUVs, knowing he'd try to upsell me to one of those. I swear he got a boner when I told him we were getting the car for Maura."

"Disgusting," Maura responded, looking like she was going to be sick.

"I know, eh?" Heather cringed with her. "When I told him we preferred an electric vehicle, I think his eyes turned to dollar signs like in a cartoon. He'd sat at his desk until then. At that point, he got up, put his arm around my shoulder and told me he had 'just the car' for me. It had arrived today and was bound to fly off the lot in no time."

"That's a classic line," Ron replied. "I have to admit I've used that with some condos." He looked around. "But only because it was true in those cases." He didn't think his siblings bought it though.

Heather politely grinned. "I shrugged my shoulders hard about five times on the way out of the building to the lot to get him to loosen his grip. The creep didn't take the hint. It felt very sleazy." She shivered in memory of it. "He took me past some cars that looked like they hadn't gotten touched up for resale yet, likely trying to make the 'car of my dreams' look even better. We got to the car and it's a nice looking Tesla. The inside is in great shape for a car that's four years old, but I sensed that something was wrong. First, the odometer had less than ten thousand kilometres on it. That's like brand new. Of course, he said it was only driven twice a week by a nice old lady – once to church and once to get groceries."

"That's like the oldest line in the book of bad car dealer lines," Kevin laughed.

"That's what I was thinking as he said it. I caught myself from doing an eyeroll!" exclaimed Heather. "I guess with me being," she used air quotes, "'a dumb broad', he could say anything." She paused to take a bite of dinner followed by a quick drink. She hummed while eating, not noticing the grins around the table. "Danny sat in the passenger seat beside me. He held up the key before giving it to me, like it's the key to the city or something. I looked at him, like, for real, dude?"

"A bit of a showman too," Ron replied. "Have to admit I do that sometimes when handing over the key to a condo after the deal closes. Of course, eye contact is important then, like you've done the customer a big favour."

"Yes!" Heather loudly replied. "My god, that stare was creepy, not congratulatory. Besides, I hadn't bought anything yet."

"Not in your eyes, maybe," Ron answered. "But to him, you're an easy mark that's good as done. You come in a few days before Christmas for a present – he knows you're not walking away empty-handed. Especially with Mom's deep pockets."

"I suppose," Heather nodded, finishing another bite. "The next warning flag was the car itself. It didn't turn over right away. He claimed it'd sat on the truck for a while and they unloaded the car without starting it. I could see they'd driven it through the car wash, as there were fresh icy tire tracks behind it. I mean, it's electric and it's not that cold out. I pretended to agree with his excuse, realizing this car likely had a history of battery issues."

"Did you get him to write it up?" Kevin anxiously asked, saying what Ron was thinking.

"Oh, my lord, was that an ordeal!" Heather sighed. "All the add-ons he slapped in there added about twenty grand. I asked him for the details. He gave me patronizing explanations for each one. I wanted to slap him silly halfway through but kept nodding like the dumb girl he thought I was."

"Did you get the maintenance insurance?" Ron asked.

"Are you kidding me? That policy is going to protect my car against *everything*! I think I'm covered if the car is destroyed by an alien attack." She laughed for a second then looked at Kevin. "Oh, by the way, if he looks at you funny tomorrow, it's probably because I asked him if the seat fabric was covered for your incontinence issues."

"Not cool, Sis," Kevin replied while the others laughed.

"Such language at the dinner table," Maura stated, grimacing.

"Sorry, Maura," Heather apologized. "This is typical dinner conversation with this group."

"Can I see the agreement?" Ron inquired.

"Sure, it's on the credenza in the foyer." She leaned her head in the direction. "And yes, I made sure I got the VIN and kilometres clearly written on the top."

"Perfect," Ron replied, his mouth half full of food.

Heather looked at Kevin. "Man was he pissed when I told him that you'd have to come in to sign for it because you had power of attorney over Mom's money. He thought he had me hook, line, and sinker. The way he pouted, you'd have thought I took his blankie away." She chuckled again. "It was very satisfying to see him sulk, for a minute anyway. Then he got creepy again. I thought he was going to grope me for a minute. I guess I'm too old for him. He asked me to tell you to bring Maura along with you so he could, and his words not mine, 'see the look of satisfaction on her face', ugh!"

Dale J. Moore

December 24th
Christmas Eve Morning

17   Mark Visits Hospital

Mark left the house early in the morning, having promised to catch up with an old friend before visiting his mother in the hospital. Parking his mother's BMW in the diner's parking lot, he approached the door with his coat unzipped. They'd experienced a blast of artic air in Calgary the past few days, and it felt mild in Windsor by comparison. Not that he usually bundled up much anyway. He was tolerant of the cold. On bitterly cold days when his labourers complained of numb fingers and toes, he'd send them home and continue to work on his own.

A waitress greeted him at the front door, a small shawl covering her shoulders to protect her from the outside draft introduced by every entering and leaving customer. Mark quickly spotted his friend, thanked the waitress, and walked over to the table, a large grin on his face.

"Doug, you old slug!" Mark reached his hand out to shake. His buddy skipped the handshake, instead pulling him forward for a bear hug.

"The Calgary Kid has returned," replied Doug, pulling back to look at his high school friend. "You don't look too bad for an old shit," he laughed, motioning his friend to sit.

"Ain't that the hole calling the porta john dirty," Mark laughed.

"Still gross, I see."

"What do you expect from a construction guy?"

"I thought you moved into sales and left the real work to the young guys," Doug said, motioning to the waitress for two fresh coffees.

"I'm the boss but I still like to get into the trenches. Not to micro-manage or anything. Just to keep my hands active. Patty does most of the paperwork. That frees me up to do some of the real work, as you call it."

"You never said what finally brought you home for a visit. I know you didn't come all this way just to have breakfast with me. Not that I'm not worth it."

"Sadly, no. Mom had an accident in the kitchen. She got burned pretty bad." He looked down at his steaming coffee.

"Sorry to hear, man."

"Thanks," Mark replied. "I'm told it's bad, but I haven't seen her yet. I'm up there after this." He paused as they ordered. "So how are things with you? Retired from Chryslers, aren't you?"

"Yeah, it's been ten years now. I do odd construction jobs, some legitimate. Mostly cash under the table stuff. Don't want those jerks in Ottawa taking it all away from me or clawing back my monthly benefits."

"Yeah, it must have been tough, retiring at fifty," Mark laughed.

His buddy grinned. "I don't miss working on the line or coming home to scrub my hands raw to get the grease off them."

Mark nodded. Though he couldn't relate to the grease issue, he dealt with constant chapped hands. "How's Betty? Did she leave your sorry ass yet?"

"I guess you never heard." Doug looked down. "She left me five years ago for the other side." He looked up at Mark. "I don't mean chicks," he forced a smile. "Cancer. Brutal it was. You think you're a badass, then something like that happens and you fall apart like cheap gloves."

"Sorry, man. Cancer is the worst. I'd rather get hit by a truck than go out like that."

"Don't you know it. If I get it, I give you permission to run me over," Doug laughed.

"Why wait?" Mark asked. "Is that your F-150 in the lot? I could do it right after we eat."

"What a buddy you are," Doug replied. "I think I'll pass for now." He shoved a strip of bacon in his mouth. Mumbling, he added, "You mentioned a favour. What is it?"

Mark left breakfast, his favour agreed to and his stomach full following a hearty morning meal. The short drive to the hospital saw his anxiety grow with each block. Not one to get queasy, his mind turned more than his stomach.

He stopped in the doorway of his mother's room, a small flower vase in his hand and a lump in his throat. The lump felt heavier. Mark took a deep breath, approaching his mother's bedside.

"Hello, Mom." He looked over her hopefully-healing body, looking for some sign of awareness on her part. "I brought you some flowers." He held them up in front of her, a couple leaves twirling free to land on her blanket. "Oh crap," he muttered. He reached down to pluck the leaves from their resting place, only to inadvertently tip the overfilled vase, causing a small stream of water over the edge onto his mother. Mark cursed at himself again. He quickly straightened the vase, yanking it away from above her. Unfortunately, his hand with the vase ran into the intravenous bag, causing it to go swaying viscously from side to side. An alarm on the machine sounded. Panicking, he extracted his arm from that area and walked over to the nearby table to set her flowers down as a nurse entered the room.

She looked startled at first, clutching her chest. "I'm sorry, I didn't realize she had a visitor."

"Sorry," Mark replied. "My arm hit the IV."

The nurse quickly reset the alarm and adjusted the intravenous setup. "No problem," she smiled, motioning with her hand. "Perhaps you should stand on the other side of the bed to talk to her."

Mark nodded, embarrassed. "Sure. Sorry to bother you."

She grinned back. "No bother. Enjoy your visit."

After the nurse left, Mark noticed the wet section on his mother's blanket remained. He ripped some paper towels from the nearby dispenser, gently dabbing them on the blanket covering her abdomen where he'd spilled the water.

"I hope this doesn't hurt, Mom." He finished wiping up the mess, balled up the tissue, then basketball style, tossed them dead centre into the corner trash can. "Nothing but net," he said. The nervous klutziness had disappeared. He found a chair and sat, wanting to rest his sore knee that ached from the flights yesterday. "I still have that bum knee. It had been pretty good until I aggravated it by taking Jack Jr. skiing. I told you his dad was taking him when we last talked. The little guy enjoyed it so much that he wanted to go again." He smiled to himself. "That kid's got more energy than a nuclear power plant. Man is he a going concern," he laughed. Then he frowned. "I guess you've never met him in person, have you." He stood, placing his hand gently on his mother's upper arm, between the upper body bandaging and her hand wraps. "I can't tell you how sorry I am that I haven't been to visit in such a long time. Life just got busy. Starting a business was more than Dad ever could have prepared me for." He looked at his mother's face; her eyes remained closed. "Then the stress of having to save the business, well, you know what we all went through there." He walked to the sink to fetch a drink of water from the tap. "All of this while trying to raise a family. I don't know how you and Dad did it so effortlessly. I never remember you guys fighting about all the crap we put you through. There were days that I thought Patty was going to skin me alive for stupid parenting." He laughed, thinking of some incidents in his head that weren't so funny at the time. "It's much less stressful being a grandparent, I can tell you that. Spoil them and send them home at the end of the day. That's what you used to say when my kids were little. Remember that? Man, it seems like forever now."

He let go of her arm and rubbed the top of his head, a look of grief overtaking his face. He paced around the room lost in his own thoughts. Finally, he stopped at her bedside. "I should have made the time. I know that now." He rubbed his hands vigorously together, like he was trying to remove a stubborn stain. "I'm truly sorry. I promise to visit more often." It sounded lame, he knew. He made a promise to himself to make sure it happened.

December 24th
Christmas Eve Morning

18   Preparations

Ron sat in the dining room to make his calls. His contact at the Ministry of Transportation looked up the VIN on the contract Heather had obtained. The car descriptions matched. The last reported mileage by the previous owner was over eighty thousand kilometres, not the ten thousand on the odometer and contract. He had his contact email him the information before he left at noon for the holiday. Ron forwarded the email to Stan, his contact at the police fraud unit.

"Stan Bishop, how are you doing?"

"Doing good. Long time no see, Ron. How's the big city treating you?"

"Good. It's a busy, crazy place and I love it," Ron responded.

"I'm surprised you didn't call me Stan the Man, like in the old days," Stan quipped.

"I'm not one to live in the old days, though I like to keep in touch with old friends. I suppose you've grown out of that name anyway."

"Yeah, the guys here now call me Stan the Con Man, since I'm in Fraud."

Ron laughed. "Makes sense." He sensed the opportunity to switch subjects. "Thanks for the voice mail this morning. Did you get my email just now with the information from the contract and the Ministry?"

"Indeed, I did. You've got us a live one here. We've investigated Danny Miller for the past few months, based on a couple of complaints. Those complaints have centred around his suspect warranty business. Proof of the odometer reset is great, but it's not the icing on the cake."

"What do you mean?" Ron asked.

"The specific car is the jackpot. I don't want to go throwing accusations around until we confirm the VIN on here matches the sale vehicle."

"How do we go about that? Does Kevin need to take a picture of the VIN when he goes to the dealership?"

"No, I have a better idea. That is, if your brother will agree to participate in a police operation."

"I was hoping you were going to say that!" Ron excitedly replied. "I only wish it were me taking part."

"Are you able to do this right away, like today?"

"Absolutely, Kevin said he's available for whatever you need. That is if you have the manpower available. It is Christmas Eve, after all."

"You're talking to the manpower," he laughed. "I'll have a unit with me, parked away from the lot." He looked at his watch. "Can I come by in an hour to run over the details with Kevin? Then we'll head straight over to the dealership."

"I'll get everyone here. We'll be ready to go."

Dale J. Moore

December 24th
Christmas Eve Day

19   *The Details*

Mark answered the call from Ron during his walk out of the hospital. He listened to his brother's excited recap of his calls.

"Got it. I'll have Doug meet us at Mom's at that time. See you soon."

It's crazy to do this on Christmas Eve.

His mind wandered back to his mother, lying helplessly in the hospital. Not much of a Christmas for her. Her family finally visits at Christmas, and she is completely unaware of their presence. He tried to console himself that he wasn't the only horrible child that never visited. All her children shared a piece of the blame. That didn't make him feel better, only worse. They'd all failed her.

Not that it made up for their absence, but he hoped that getting Danny Miller out of her hair would provide some measure of apology. Perhaps it would start a sort of family healing process. Lord knows they hadn't acted much like a family for the past ten years. His mind went back to Danny's extortion. How could they not have known this was going on for so long? Not the kind of thing for his mother to bring up on their regular phone calls, he guessed. Whenever possible, he avoided discussing anything bad on those calls, not wanting to upset his mother.

105

He needed to share some things, but he often deferred a topic until a resolution had already occurred. Like Maggie's broken arm skiing – he didn't tell his mother about that for two weeks. He always feared she'd overreact and jump on the next plane. Perhaps another resolution for the new year was more honesty on those calls, though he sensed his mother knew when he wasn't exactly truthful and glossed over issues. Mothers had that sixth sense, didn't they? He'd seen it with Patty and their kids.

Pulling up to his mother's home, he was taken aback by the number of vehicles in the driveway and on the street, including a police cruiser. With the double driveway blocked, he parked his vehicle on the road. He walked into the house to see two police officers standing, hands on hips, in the foyer. His family and his friend Doug sat on the couches. Another man stood in front of them. Stan from Fraud, he assumed, though his attire said 'mechanic'.

"Great, you're here," Stan reached forward to shake hands. "Stan Bishop, nice to meet you, Mark."

"Same," Mark nodded and shook his hand. He stood in front of a recliner at the end of one of the couches.

"We've run through the details already, Mark. Since you don't have an active role, I thought you wouldn't mind. Doug has explained how you think he could help. I think it's perfect. An unfamiliar face will help with the diversion." Stan looked around the room. "Any questions?" He paused. He checked his watch. "I've got twelve-fifteen." He looked up to see nodding heads. "Good. Kevin. You and Maura can leave as soon as you're ready. I'll follow you and arrive a couple of minutes after. I'll let you get through introductions and get Miller comfortable."

"Okay," Kevin replied. He looked at Maura. "I need a quick visit to the bathroom then we can go."

Maura nodded, indicating her readiness.

"Good." Stan turned to the uniforms. "You park down the block. Wait for my call. If you don't hear anything within thirty minutes from the time we enter Millers Motors, do a casual drive-by. I don't expect any trouble, but protocols, you know."

The officers nodded, leaving for their unit.

Stan talked to Ron and Mark. "Thanks for your help with the information and setup. This will make a nice Christmas present for the boss." He looked at Ron. "I'm sure Kevin will give you the recap when he returns. Feel free to call me if you have questions. Maybe wait until Boxing Day though. Doing the paperwork after this little sting will likely keep me tied up to past the point where my wife will be happy when I get home. She'll wring my neck if I take any calls on Christmas Day since I'm supposed to have it off work."

"Good luck," Ron replied, shaking hands goodbye.

Dale J. Moore

December 24th
Christmas Eve Day

20   Millers Motors

"I feel half dressed," Maura complained. The conservative dresser wiggled in the car seat in a futile attempt to tug her short skirt down just a bit.

"Your skirt is almost to your knees," Kevin replied, giving her legs a quick glance.

"I know, but I almost always wear pants. If I don't, I'm wearing a long dress." She pointed to her feet. "Down to here."

"I'm sorry to make you feel uncomfortable. We want you to distract Danny. If he drools all over you in your cleaning outfit, just imagine what that skirt will do to him. Just don't let him bother you. Ignore whatever sleazeball things come out of his mouth. Let me do most of the talking. Okay?"

Maura nodded, her hands covering her knees.

Parking in the lot of Millers Motors, Kevin grabbed the contract from the back seat, folding it to slip into his coat pocket. They walked by a Tesla, parked near the front door.

"That's likely the car," remarked Kevin.

"It's a nice car," remarked Maura. "Not really my colour. For free, I won't complain." She grinned at Kevin.

He laughed, opening the dealership door for her. Music played and heads turned toward the door briefly. Walking into the main showroom, their attention was drawn to the sound of a falling chair. They looked to their left to see Danny picking his chair off the ground.

"Told you the skirt would work," Kevin grinned at Maura.

Done with the chair, Danny tucked in his shirt then took a swipe to straighten his hair with his bare hand. He glanced at his reflection on the glass door as he passed.

"Kevin Montgomery," Danny leaned in close to shake his hand.

Kevin shook his hand. "Danny. You remember Maura, don't you?"

"How could I forget," Danny replied. He looked her up and down, more down at her legs. "You look pretty damn hot," Danny said, drool practically flowing from the corners of his mouth.

"Thank you," Maura timidly replied.

"So, we're getting you a car today. How exciting!" Danny exclaimed, rubbing his hands together, leaving the land of the leering into selling mode. "The car's right out front," he pointed to the car they'd passed. He pointed the keys at the car to unlock the doors. We can take a quick look now, or if you don't want to waste your time, I've got the copies set out for your signatures."

"We'll look it over. We're just waiting for a friend of mine," Kevin began to say.

At that moment, Stan walked through the front doors, wearing his mechanic coveralls.

Danny stopped, turning to raise his voice at him. "How many times I have told you guys? Mechanics do not use the front door."

Danny moved his finger up and down pointing at Stan. "We don't want you grease monkeys anywhere near our customers!"

Kevin put his hand up in a stopping motion toward Danny as he stepped toward Stan. "I'm sorry, Danny. He's with me. This is Stan. He's going to give the car a once-over before we sign."

Danny's jaw dropped, not used to such a request from clients. "I'm not sure I can allow that." He mumbled to himself for a minute. "Health and Safety issue. Yes, that's it. It's a Health and Safety issue. I can't let outside mechanics work on the cars." Racking his brain for excuses, he added, "My insurance doesn't allow it either, I think."

"He's not going to work on the car. He just wants to look it over. He's a friend from way back, doing me a favour."

Stan reached forward to shake Danny's hand. "Stan," he simply stated.

Danny looked at the hands that Stan had purposely dirtied, cringing to avoid the handshake. "Nice to meet you," he said without any conviction as he patted the mechanic on his arm. "Let's get those papers signed, then you can look all you want."

Kevin's eyebrows wrinkled. "That doesn't make any sense. What's the point of looking it over after you buy it?"

"It's not my rules. It's the government's rules."

Stan stared him down. "I've never heard of such a rule."

"Well of course not," Danny smirked condescendingly at Stan. "You're just a mechanic. What do you know of laws?"

Kevin could see Stan beginning to fume. Now he had both Maura and Stan ready to kill Danny. He had to calm the situation or risk blowing the whole plan. "No problem," Kevin told Danny. "We'll look inside, maybe pop the hood. No touching the engine or anything."

Stan caught on. "Sounds good. I don't know these electrical contraptions anyway. I'm more curious than I'm sure I can help."

Danny backed off, satisfied that Stan was an idiot who wouldn't find any problems.

As the group walked out the door, a large, black luxury SUV pulled into the lot, the midday sun blaring off the polished finish. Danny stopped in his tracks, the sound of money ringing in his head.

"You guys go ahead and take a look." He tossed the key to Kevin. "I better see what this customer needs." Danny straightened up, marching over to the new arrival, ready to sell.

Kevin chuckled to himself. He watched as Mark's friend Doug, wearing his best suit, stepped out of the vehicle. When Danny got close, Doug rolled up his sleeve to expose the Rolex he'd borrowed from Ron.

"Let's go," Kevin said to Stan. "Doug will talk him up for a bit, then start looking at the most expensive vehicles on the lot."

Stan quickly found the VIN, taking a picture with his phone to compare it to the contract number. They matched. He went around to the front of the car and lifted the hood. He glanced around the engine. "It looks like there was a fire in here," he pointed out to Kevin while snapping more photos.

Maura leaned in, not knowing about cars but recognizing the singe marks along one side of the engine that Danny's cleaners had missed removing.

"I see what you mean," Kevin acknowledged.

Stan glanced at Danny to see if he was looking their way. Doug had Danny tied up in discussion, his hands waving animatedly in the air. Doug had shifted positions such that Danny faced away from the Tesla. Stan dropped to his knees, then onto his back to slide his head under the belly of the car. "Whoa, it looks a lot worse under here. I don't think they even tried to clean up down here." Stan grunted as he wiggled his shoulders under the frame to snap some more images. He stood up, dusting off his overalls' knees and butt. He closed the hood of the car, drawing a quick glance from Danny. Stan gave him a thumbs up, accompanied by a stupid grin.

"Are you sure this thing even starts?" Stan asked Kevin.

"Heather said it was slow to turn over but did eventually."

"I'm surprised it started at all, based on the reports from the insurance company," Stan replied.

Kevin gave him a puzzled look.

They heard a heavy door slam behind them. They turned to see Doug get back in his shimmering SUV. Danny strutted toward them like a male peacock.

"Like selling candy to kids," Danny laughed.

"Got a nibble, did you?" Kevin asked.

"More than a nibble. The dude's looking to buy two high-end SUVs right after Christmas. Happy flipping New Year to me!" Danny proclaimed, looking skyward, like the Lord favoured him.

Kevin went along, all the while knowing Doug had no intention of buying anything but had provided the necessary distraction.

"We looked over the car." Kevin looked at Maura. "We're ready to sign the papers."

"It's so exciting," Maura added, clasping her hands while she jumped up and down a bit.

"Great," Danny grinned, fish on the line. "Follow me."

As they headed inside, Stan spotted the patrol car and gave them the signal to circle around one more time.

Danny sat in his leather high-back chair, with Kevin and Maura in the guest chairs. Stan stood in the doorway, leaning on the frame, arms crossed.

"Alright, just a few more things to discuss to finalize the paperwork," Danny said, pulling brochures from his desk. He slid one across the desk to Kevin. "I know you want to do the right thing when it comes to giving Maura a gift worthy of the support she's given your mother, so I went ahead and had the ultimate rustproofing applied to the exterior and undercarriage, as well as the maximum seat protective spray applied. If you look at this revised contract, you'll see the costs for those here," and he pointed to one 'x', "and here," and he pointed to a second 'x'. "Just initial those and we're good."

Kevin turned to look at Stan, knowing what Danny had said he did was illegal without consent. He also knew that neither he nor Stan smelled the supposed protections applied and the odor would have lingered inside and outside of the vehicle so soon afterward.

Stan shrugged, nodding to Kevin to play along while making a mental note to add charging for non-applied services to the list.

"Great," Danny said after Kevin initialed. "Now for the most important part of your purchase. That is what we call," he hesitated to hold up a glossy pamphlet, almost expecting a drum roll, "the Miller Piller, our best in the business bumper-to-bumper warranty."

Kevin looked at the glossy brochure. "Shouldn't it be Pillar, with an 'a'? Like a strong support."

Danny looked at him. "No, it's an 'e' in piller."

"Piller with an 'e' is an old word that means thief," Kevin explained.

"e, a, what's the diff, eh?" He laughed at his words. "It's the best you can buy. Period. End of sentence. End of story. Mic drop, like the kids say today." Danny pushed himself back in his chair, holding up his clenched hands then opening them quickly as he loudly said, "Boom!"

Kevin chuckled at the theatrics. *What a clown.* Thief was right he thought, looking at the prices.

Maura glanced at the brochure. "It seems like there are a lot of asterisks besides what the agreement covers. What do those mean?"

Danny gave her a condescending look. "Don't you worry your pretty little head about those. That's just technical guy stuff you wouldn't understand." He looked at the mechanic in the doorway. "Standard stuff, am I right?"

"I can't see it from here." Stan looked at Maura, giving a slight wink that Danny didn't catch. "As Mr. Miller pointed out, I'm no lawyer but I'm sure he'd stand by his agreement in the face of the law."

Danny looked at him, briefly concerned but letting it pass. "Of course, I stand by all my contracts."

"Great," Kevin said. "We'll take the all-inclusive option."

Danny almost fell off the chair in surprise. Nobody took the all-inclusive option, no matter how hard his upsell. "Sure, no problem." He leaned forward, scrambling for a pen before Kevin could change his mind. "Let me just tweak those numbers." Danny scribbled on the contract and altered the final numbers. "There. Ready for initials, then final signature!" he exclaimed.

Kevin looked back at Stan. "There was something you wanted me to add, right?"

"Yeah, it's just a little thing," Stan said, looking at Danny. "Just add a line at the bottom saying the batteries are the manufacturer originals. It's important to have OEM parts in a car, especially when it comes to repairs. I'm sure a smart businessman like yourself agrees with that, Mr. Miller."

Danny scrunched his face and replied flippantly, "Of course, any idiot knows that."

Stan left his leaning post, pulling the contract toward him on the corner of the desk. He picked up the pen, leaned forward, and wrote the line down. Stan straightened, turned the contract back toward Danny, then reached out to hand the pen back.

Danny looked at the pen, disgusted by the thought of touching the grease-monkey-handled pen. He pulled open his desk drawer, yanking out a sanitary wipe. He cleaned the pen up and down about five times, then tossed the wipe into the garbage pail beside his desk. Danny didn't read past the first few words of the added sentence.

"Just initial it, then I will," Kevin added. "And just initial where I initialed to confirm mine." He waited for Danny to complete the task. "And just one by the odometer reading and VIN number, for my insurance." Danny quickly scribbled his initials.

"Great," Kevin said. "While you have the pen, you might as well sign it, then I will."

Danny signed, then leaned back, revelling in a massive profit, with more expected later from the sucker who'd come into the lot earlier.

Kevin picked up the pen. He leaned forward to sign the contract when Stan spoke up.

"Don't sign that." He pulled out his phone. "Now, boys."

The police car pulled into the lot, lights flashing. Two uniformed officers quickly stepped out.

"What's going on here?" Danny yelled at Stan.

"Yeah, what's going on?" Kevin reiterated, feigning confusion.

"Danny Miller, you are under arrest for fraud over five thousand dollars." Stan held up his badge.

"What? I'm trying to make a living here," Danny complained.

Kevin shrugged. "What about my car?" he asked Stan, playing along. "You're not a mechanic, are you?"

"No, that was a ruse, sorry," Stan replied. "That car is evidence. You wouldn't want that particular car anyway, trust me. You and the young lady may leave now."

"This is a joke, right?" Danny asked Stan, glancing at Kevin for support.

Kevin shrugged his shoulders, eyebrows raised like he was as startled as Danny by what had happened.

"No joke," replied Stan, reaching for his handcuffs.

117

A look of panic struck Danny's face. Surprisingly, he ran toward Stan, taking a swing at him as he passed. Stan ducked. Danny's fist hit the glass door behind Stan. Danny tried to bolt out the door, but Stan stuck out his leg, causing Danny to trip. He hit the floor with a thud, complemented with the painful sound of air leaving Danny's chest. He lay there moaning, looking up at Stan.

"This is a waste of your time," Danny argued, gasping for breath, struggling only slightly against the officer cuffing him. "I've had these contract issues thrown out of court before."

"Maybe, but now we've got assaulting an officer to add to the charges," Stan added, jerking on Danny's shoulder to get the cuffed man to stand.

Danny yanked his shoulder, freeing himself from Stan's grasp, but with no hands to put in front of himself to brace for his fall, he face-planted on the tile floor.

"Done?" Stan asked Danny, lying crumpled on the floor.

Danny protested some more, though it sounded like whining. "You can't treat me like this. I've got cameras all around the dealership, you know."

"Perfect," Stan replied. "I'll make sure I get that video before I leave too."

"It will never stick. I'll get out before midnight," Danny proclaimed loudly as he was escorted through the showroom.

"I don't think so. Not this time," Stan replied. "Aside from taking a swing at me, you made another big mistake on this one."

Danny looked at him. "What are you talking about?"

"The car you sold him. It was illegal to sell it for anything but scrap parts." He stared down Danny. "But you knew that all along. That car had a defective battery array. The car was written off by the insurance company because it would cost more to replace the batteries than to buy a new car. That is fraud, plain and simple. I think you're looking at time behind bars."

Dale J. Moore

December 24th
Christmas Eve Afternoon

21   An Eventful Trip

With no involvement in the car dealership sting operation, Ron and
Heather headed to the hospital for another visit. Mark had some urgent
work issues to deal with over the phone, telling the others he'd see them
later. They decided to take their mother's Jeep, Ron afraid of parking
his new toy in a crowded lot.

The drive downtown gave Ron and Heather some time to catch
up.

"How do you stand it?" Heather asked her brother.

"Stand what?" Ron inquired.

"The crowds, the hustle, the subway, driving on those parking
lots they call highways. All of it." She flailed her arms around. "I don't
know how I did it, looking back. And that was what? Over twenty-five
years ago. It's even crazier now!"

"Are you kidding?" He looked at his sister. "That's the beauty
of the city," he laughed, then paused. "Well, maybe not sitting in
traffic."

"I can't even drive in Windsor traffic," Heather lamented.

"The people downtown are what gives Toronto its energy." He
rotated his hands as they gripped the steering wheel. "I step out into the

streets and just soak it up. I can feel it course through my body. It's hard to describe," he said, grasping the steering wheel tight. "When I come back from the quiet of the cottage, it's like I've been starving for days." He glanced at his sister, his eyes wide with excitement. "Back in the city, I've got an all-you-can-eat buffet of social activity. The buzz of the streets, the clamour of the subway, the vibe of the bars. Energy everywhere."

"Wow!" Heather replied, staring at Ron. "That's intense. I can't say I ever thought about Toronto like that, even when I lived there."

"You did live with that asshole. That might have had something to do with it."

"There is that," Heather grinned.

"So, why did you turn into miss Hallmark Channel small-town environment healer?"

Heather laughed. "You make it sound like a bad thing."

"Isn't it?" Ron smirked.

"Mary told me I needed to change, for my mental and physical health. I agreed but didn't expect such extreme change. Can I tell you something I never told her?"

"Sure, I think?" Ron hesitantly replied, never one for touchy-feely, sensitive conversation with anyone other than his wife.

"The first month that I moved to B.C., I cried every night. I thought I had made a mistake. Too drastic of a change. You know?" She looked at him.

"It was a huge change, one that I couldn't make," he remarked.

"I barely slept – it was too quiet. I missed the background noise of the city." She looked over, laughing. "I don't have that issue anymore." She turned solemn. "I missed having someone there, even if he was a total loser. I'd never lived alone before. When I moved to T.O., friends put me up. I met dork-face within a few weeks and moved in with him. It was whirlwind, for sure."

"It's a challenge, growing up in a big family, watching everyone else leave the nest before you. I know I was scared when I left for Toronto. I didn't know anyone. My roommate was some random guy from a notice board listing in the university cafeteria that was moving there at the same time after graduating. Didn't know him from Adam. It didn't take me long to realize that I didn't want to know him. Fortunately, back then, a bachelor apartment was affordable on starting-out wages."

"I didn't know how to escape. Until Mary helped. That's probably the only reason I stuck it out after that first month out west. I didn't want to let Mary down. It all worked out, but the first year was bumpy as hell."

"I don't think you could have ever let Mary down. She would apologize and would have come up with a Plan B for you. Knowing her, she had a Plan B in her back pocket before you moved out there."

The two Montgomery kids sat at their mother's bedside for a few hours, talking with her a bit, but mostly reminiscing about old times. Heather felt the warmth of family in those years-old tales. The time flew by before Ron looked at the window to see darkness descending. He looked at his watch.

"Wow, it's half past five. We better get heading home."

123

"Sh…," Heather started to say, covering her mouth. She still thought it disrespectful to swear in front of her mother. Putting their coats on, she asked. "Do you think we have time to drive along the river then swing home?"

"Sure. I think we said around seven o'clock for dinner," Ron replied, waiting for the elevator. "I haven't seen the Detroit skyline in quite some time. I hear the Joe is gone."

The elevator opened. They waited for a few new visitors and a nurse to exit before they entered and resumed their conversation.

"They were talking about bringing it down last time I was here," Heather replied. "I hear the new arena is awesome."

"It looks good on television. Maybe on another visit I can get over there."

Arriving at their car, Ron said he was going to head a bit east first, then north to the river. He wanted to see more of the lit up waterfront. Ron took a route through some older downtown streets. Homeless people manned a few corners looking for a handout. Others began hunkering down for the night.

"It's a shame that there are still homeless people in this world," Heather sighed.

"You should see some sections of Toronto. I guess it's like that in any city though. The bigger the city, the bigger the problem, it seems."

"Look at that guy over there," Heather pointed out as they sat waiting for a green light. Under the cover of a loading dock to an abandoned office building, lay a homeless man on a discarded stained mattress. He'd come into possession of several blankets which he struggled to use to protect himself from the oncoming cold night. The blankets looked as ragged as the clothes he tried to cover. A pile of garbage collected in the corner, not ten feet from his head.

Ron shook his head. "I struggle to understand how that happens with all the social programs we have in place. Not to mention the booming economy."

"Some people don't want handouts; others waste that money on booze and drugs. Some just can't get the handouts, as you call them."

"Why can't this guy get a job? I've never gone without a job since I was sixteen."

"Really?" Heather questioned. "You had everything you needed when you were young. You took advantage of it. Who knows what this guy's story is, how he got here."

The light changed. "And we're not staying to find out either," Ron remarked. He cruised through the intersection. A few minutes later they turned down Walker Road toward the river. They crossed the train tracks, noting that the train was still boarding for Toronto. Turning onto Riverside Drive, Ron noted the former Hiram Walker buildings.

"Who owns this now?" Ron asked.

"I don't know. I've lost track. I think they still make Canadian Club here but also make Wisers and some other booze."

"That reminds me, I need to stop at the LCBO for some whisky."

"I think there's an LCBO downtown if you want to quickly stop in there. Hopefully they are still open."

They slowly drove along the river, admiring the lights of the Detroit skyline across the still flowing and glistening river. The reflections from the tall buildings on the other side spread across the water, like they reached for the Canadian shore. The RenCen and Blue Cross buildings were easy to recognize on the other shore. Casino Windsor lit up the Windsor skyline. Crossing Ouellette Avenue, Heather pointed.

"Just up here, past the museum."

"What is that?" Ron asked about a glass-looking structure set behind the museum.

"It's an Olympic size pool and kids' water area. Mom showed it to me last time I was here. Didn't go in it, though." She paused as Ron slowed to look at it. "We want to turn here, just past the bus station."

"I forgot that had moved too," he looked it over. "Looks good. The old one was grimy."

Approaching the LCBO, they noticed the lack of lights.

"Crap," Ron said. "Closed. I guess I'll have to drink Mom's booze."

"That was never a problem when you were seventeen," Heather laughed.

"Sixteen," Ron grinned, "but who's counting?"

As Ron pulled up to the corner by the LCBO, Heather called out. "Did you see that girl back there?"

"Maybe. You mean the homeless one up against the wall of the LCBO?"

"Yes, that one. We need to go back."

"What do you mean go back?"

"Something's not right. I need to go back to take another look at her."

"Okay," Ron said, looking around. "Let me finish the turn and park on Wyandotte. We can walk over and look. Just stay close to me. It's dark and we don't know this area anymore."

They walked back around the corner from the parked Jeep, passing the front doors of the old LCBO. They could see a young woman huddled up against the wall.

"Keep your distance, Heather. She could be dangerous, especially if startled."

"I don't think she belongs here," Heather replied, giving the girl a once-over.

"None of them belong here, now do they?" Ron asked. "Didn't you just say that?"

"No, I mean look at her. She's in new clean clothes."

Ron looked closer. "I see what you mean. You don't see many homeless wearing Canada Goose coats. Unless they stole them, of course."

"She's just got a look," Heather added. She took a few approaching steps closer. "Excuse me," she said to the girl.

No sign of movement.

Heather cleared her throat. "Ahem, excuse me," she repeated, much louder than the first time.

The young girl looked up, startled. "Leave me alone!" she replied, more sad than angry.

Ron pulled on Heather's arm, a signal to leave. Heather pulled her arm away.

"I'm not going to hurt you," Heather said a bit softer. "You look lost."

"She's probably coming off a bender," Ron replied.

The girl rolled over then stood up, dusting herself off. Although mascara smudged her face, they could tell she was a beautiful young woman. She ran her fingers through her hair in a feeble attempt to return it to normal state. "I am not coming off a bender." She began to cry.

Heather took a step toward her before feeling Ron's hand once more on her arm. She turned and glared at her brother. He pulled his hand back and raised both hands in an 'I surrender' pose. He stayed where he was, ready to help if needed.

"Are you injured?" Heather quietly asked.

"Not physically," the girl replied.

"What's your name?" Heather asked her.

"Mary," came the meek reply.

Heather grinned. "That was my sister's name."

"Was?" Mary asked.

"Yes, she died ten years ago. Cancer," Heather said, fighting back a tear. Just saying it sometimes was trigger enough.

"I'm sorry," Mary responded, looking down at the ground.

"Thanks," Heather answered. "How did a nice girl like you end up sleeping beside an LCBO?"

"I went for a late lunch downtown with Mom. It was going fine until the usual argument came up about 'what am I going to do with my life'."

Heather glanced at Ron, sympathetic toward the young woman. Mary's eyes and complexion made her look like a teenager. "What happened?"

"I grabbed my coat and ran out of the restaurant, leaving my mother sitting there. I had to get out of there. It felt like the walls were closing in around me. You know what I mean?"

"I know what you mean," Heather replied.

"I can't deal with that pressure right now. At Christmas," Mary continued. "We should be doing family things that bring us together, not pull us apart."

Heather agreed with the sentiment. She stayed silent, realizing that she did not know the situation enough to comment. She made sure Ron didn't say anything either. She loved her brother, but he could say some stupid, insensitive things at times.

"In my hurry to get out of there, I left my purse. My phone was dead when I left the house. I only charged it for a few minutes on the car ride downtown. Of course, my charger was in my purse, hanging on the back of the restaurant chair."

"I see," said a concerned Heather.

"In my stupidity, I drained what little power I had calling a girlfriend. The phone died mid-call."

"How can we help?"

Mary held out her phone. "Have you got a charger in your car? I'd like to call my Dad."

Heather took the phone and handed it to Ron, who looked at the type of phone, shaking his head 'no', handing the lifeless device back.

"Ron can lend you his phone, can't you, Ron?"

Ron looked at Heather like she was crazy. All his contacts — his life — were on his phone.

Heather tilted her head, motioning toward Mary.

Ron sighed, then reluctantly turned his phone over to Mary. Having listened to the girl talk, he guessed it would be okay. He just hoped Heather was right and the girl didn't take off with the phone or smash it on the LCBO wall. It would be a bitch to go through the holidays without a phone.

"You know your dad's number, Mary?"

"Yes, I think so. Thank you."

Mary plugged in her father's number. "I hope he answers. Sometimes he doesn't answer numbers he doesn't know." She waited for a few rings, anxious until she heard him answer.

"I'm okay. Cold, but I'm okay." She listened. "A nice woman leant me her phone. It's her husband's phone."

Heather laughed. "Brother."

"Sorry," Mary smiled, finally. "Brother's phone." She listened again. "Yes, I'm safe. My phone died. How's Chris?" She listened some more. "Okay, I suppose that's fine." She handed the phone over to Heather.

"Me?" a startled Heather asked.

Mary nodded.

"Hello, Heather Stanley here."

A deep gravelly voice came from the other end of the line. "Hello, Miss Stanley,"

"Mrs.," Heather corrected.

"My apologies. This is Bernard Larocque. Where are you right now?"

"We're downtown at the LCBO. Do you know where it is?"

"I think so. I'm out by Harrow."

"Maybe we could meet you partway" She looked at Mary. "I mean if that's okay with you and Mary."

"What'd you have in mind?" Mary's father asked.

"Give me a second to talk to my brother, he's driving." She talked it over with Ron. "He remembers passing a little plaza on Dougall, just before it heads to the 401. Do you know where that is?"

"Yes," he replied. "That works. I can get there in twenty minutes or so. Can I talk to Mary again please?"

Mary took the phone back. She answered with a few 'uh-huhs', 'yes, Dads', and one 'yes I'll jump out if there's trouble', accompanied by an eyeroll toward Heather. She turned to Ron. "What's the vehicle and plate?"

"It's a Jeep," Ron replied, then realized that neither he nor Heather knew the plate number for their mother's vehicle. "It's our mom's car. Keep talking to your dad and we'll walk over to the car to see the plate, okay?"

Mary nodded and the threesome proceeded around the corner and toward the Jeep. Mary read the plate number to her father, then hung up. The group got in the car, Mary and Heather in the back, Heather teasing Ron about being a good chauffeur.

Dale J. Moore

December 24th
Christmas Eve Twilight

22   The Drive from Downtown

Heather and Mary Larocque chatted comfortably in the back seat of the car. Ron quietly drove them to their South Windsor destination.

"It's been a long day," Mary replied, looking exhausted.

"I bet you're hungry too." Heather looked kindly at her companion.

"A little. At least I'm warm now."

Heather pulled a couple of pre-moistened makeup sheets from her purse, along with a compact. "Here, you probably want to clean up a bit too. It will make you feel better."

"Thank you." Mary took the wipes and freshened up. "That does feel better."

Even in the poor lighting of the back seat, Heather could see that Mary was pretty – and young. "If you don't mind me asking, how old are you?"

"Twenty-three. Twenty-four in March."

"Why is your mother pushing you about 'doing something with your life'? Are you having trouble finding a job?" Heather paused, worried she sounded like Mary's mother. "If you don't mind me asking, of course."

"It's okay," Mary responded. "I have a part-time job, twenty hours a week."

"That's not too shabby," Heather replied. "I know many companies only hire part-time these days."

"She wants me to go to college. I don't think I can manage school on top of work and Christopher."

"Who's Christopher?" Heather asked.

"My son. He just turned six in the fall."

The response shocked Heather. She could hardly believe the young girl beside her was twenty-three, let alone had a six-year-old son.

"Don't worry," Mary grinned. "I've seen that look of surprise on people's faces plenty of times. I have a young face. The pregnancy came during my last year of high school. A graduation present, of sorts."

"That's exciting that you have a boy. What did you get him for Christmas?"

Sadness filled Mary's eyes. "Nothing, yet. Mom and I were supposed to go shopping for him after lunch …"

Ron interrupted from the front seat, as he pulled into the drug store parking lot at their destination.

"Do you see your dad's truck?" he asked Mary, his head on a swivel, scanning the mostly bare parking lot. He checked his watch. "We're a few minutes early."

"No, I don't. You can just leave me here. I'll wait for him," the young mother replied.

"In this cold? Isn't once in a day enough?" Heather asked. Without waiting for an answer, she continued. "Come on, let's you and I go into the store to get that son of yours a gift for Christmas. Ron can stay watch for your father."

"I've got no money," Mary sheepishly replied.

"My treat, or if it makes you feel better, you can pay me back later. Come on." Heather opened her door, "Let's go. They might close soon. It is Christmas Eve, after all." She didn't wait for a response, the sound of her closing door the next noise heard in the parking lot.

Mary followed suit, scurrying to catch up. "What can we possibly get in a drug store?"

"Have you not shopped in one of these stores in a while?" Heather asked, looking back as Mary caught up at the sliding entrance door. "I was in one yesterday in LaSalle. They have everything these days. I suggest we start by looking in their electronics section over by the cashier. Sound good?"

Mary agreed. They quickly found a game that Mary knew Chris would love. Heather told her the cost wasn't a problem. The cashier set it aside while they picked up a few other small toys and some chocolate for the boy's stocking.

"What about your mom and dad? Do you have anything for them?"

"Dad, yes. He's the easiest to buy for. I got my mom a new wallet but wanted to get something else small."

"What about some lipstick or costume jewelry? Inexpensive, and always needed," Heather stated.

"Sounds good."

They found something quickly and headed toward the cashier. Walking by the windows at the front, they spotted a truck pull up beside the Jeep.

"That's my dad!" Mary exclaimed, pulling on Heather's coat to hurry her along.

"You go ahead," Heather implored her. "I'll pay for this then be right out, okay?"

Mary excitedly nodded, taking a step toward the doorway. She stopped to rush back to Heather. Mary wrapped her arms around Heather in a heartfelt embrace. She whispered, "Thank you."

As Heather paid for the items and bought a reuseable bag to carry them, she could see Mary hug her father in the parking lot. It looked like she never wanted to let go. Heather sighed, knowing her sister Mary had had that same relationship with her father – a type of closeness she never shared with their father, but enjoyed with her mother. Heather prayed that this Mary could heal the relationship with her own mother, realizing that her father probably was pivotal in making that happen. She assumed the boy's father wasn't in the picture. She often wondered what her life would have been like if she'd left Jeff when he first rejected the pregnancy. Could she have made it as a single mother? How would her parents have handled it? In hindsight, knowing that staying in the relationship had cost her the chance to raise a child she bore, it wouldn't have been a difficult decision. Every time she got sad like this thinking about her loss, she thought of Kyle, and that she wouldn't have him if her life had been different. Nature's way of maintaining balance.

Exiting the building, Heather caught a wave from Mary, whose other arm still clung to her father.

"Here you go, Mary," Heather grinned warmly, handing over the shopping bag.

"What do I owe you?" Mr. Larocque inquired.

"Consider it a Christmas gift from the Montgomery family," Heather replied, looking at Ron.

"We don't take charity," Mary's father gruffly replied, straightening his back in defiance.

"It's not charity. Mary is now my friend, and it is a gift, from one friend to another."

"I insist," came the reply, stronger still.

"Ron," Heather said to her brother, "give Mary's dad one of your business cards. You two can work it out over email." She turned to Mr. Larocque. "Is that acceptable?"

He nodded, calming down. "We better get going," he said, looking down at his daughter from his six-foot-four frame. "Your mother has made herself sick with worry all day. But don't you worry. She's not angry with you. Your mom and I had a good talk today while we drove around downtown looking for you. I think it will get better between you two. I really do."

Mary grinned up to her father's teary eyes, pushing herself closer to him. "Thanks, Dad. I will do better too."

Ron handed Bernard Larocque a business card and shook his hand, wishing him and his family a merry Christmas.

Heather and Mary embraced, both shedding tears over their brief, possibly life-changing for Mary, friendship.

137

As the Larocque truck pulled out of the lot, followed by Ron and Heather in their Jeep, Ron turned to his sister.

"Well, I didn't expect that today," he said, turning and smiling at his sister. "You reminded me of our Mary today. That's exactly the kind of selfless thing she would do all the time."

Heather blushed, then shed more tears from her already swollen eyes. "I never thought of that. You're right. I guess she did rub off on me a bit."

"Mom would be proud too," Ron added, looking around to make a left turn.

"Thanks," Heather laughed. "Now you're just trying to make me cry, aren't you?"

Ron laughed. "Maybe, but it's true. I could never do anything like that. I guess the sales guy in me is always battling with the charitable guy in me. Charity guy won the battle with Christmas bonuses this year, but it's not always the case." He looked at Mary, the flow of tears finally vanquished. "Of course, Sharon helps me slay my greedy side when it rears its ugly head." He paused. "Sometimes, anyways," he laughed.

Heather smiled at her brother, putting a hand softly on his right arm from her passenger seat. "I know you're not the big bad sales guy that Mark makes you out to be. I know there's a heart in there … somewhere." She laughed again.

"Speaking of Mary, did you notice what I noticed about tonight?" Ron turned to face his sister, shock on his face.

"My god, how could I not?" she replied, sitting up straight in her seat. "I mean, what are the odds?"

"Yeah, I know right?" Ron gripped the steering wheel tightly. "We meet a young woman named Mary, who had a child right after finishing high school," he recapped, hands now frantically waving in the air. "And she names the boy Christopher. It's exactly like our sister Mary and her boy. I could barely contain myself." He finally exhaled, the odds of it all exhausting him.

"The boy's father didn't stick around in this case. Likely better for her, it seems like," Heather added. "He sounded like a loser like Danny Miller."

"I hope it works out for her," Ron replied. "I know some single mothers. They all say how hard it is some days."

"All parenting has its ups and downs. I can't imagine doing it without Barry." Heather looked out the window as they neared their mother's neighbourhood. "Let's hope today was the low point of her parenting roller coaster."

Ron glanced at his sister. "You know what I can't get out of my head?"

"I think I can guess," Heather replied.

"Okay, guess."

"That today's Mary has a six-year-old son named Christopher, and our Mary's Christopher died at six years old?"

He looked at her, surprised. "Exactly. You are getting more like our Mary." He squeezed on the steering wheel, slowly turning onto their mother's street. "I hope he doesn't meet the same fate."

Heather smiled and reassuringly placed her hand on his arm. "I'm pretty sure that won't happen. I asked Mary. Her Christopher is afraid of heights."

December 24th
Christmas Eve

23   At Home

While Mark paced back and forth in the living room, his siblings sat on the couches with Maura. He attentively listened to every detail of the retelling of each group's adventures. He had plenty of questions.

"I talked to Doug before you guys returned from Millers Motors. He said he should thank *me* for asking him to help. He said he hadn't had that much fun bullshitting someone in forever. And Doug is a born bullshitter." Mark smirked. "Do you know what they charged Danny with, or how long he may go away for?"

Kevin replied. "They haven't charged him yet. When he is, he'll be facing multiple counts of fraud over five thousand dollars. Stan says they are taking their time because they have other older complaints that they are going to dig through." He took a drink of Coke, looking satisfied from the drink and his day. "And of course, there's the other big charge to process."

"What's that?" Mark stopped pacing to ask, not aware of anything else.

Maura responded. "I sent the detective the video from your mother's security camera in the foyer. That creep Danny is now facing sexual assault charges too."

"Wow!" Mark exclaimed, resuming his pacing. "That's two serious charges against him. Sounds like he's going to be out of Mother's hair for a while."

"That was the plan," replied Kevin. "And amazingly, the plan actually worked! How often does that happen?" He laughed, nodding at Maura. "It was a good team effort, that's for sure." He turned his attention to his pacing brother. "Your buddy Doug did great. He kept Danny tied up long enough for Stan to verify what he needed. Not to mention," he added, "he got Danny thinking about a bigger sale and not paying attention to our little scam."

"I'm glad it all worked out," Mark said, stopping to shake Kevin's hand for a job well done. "It's a relief thinking Mom" — he looked across the room — "and Maura won't have to deal with that slimeball ex-brother-in-law of ours anymore."

Maura smiled, relieved over not having to open the door once a month to see Danny's weaselly face.

Ron's phone loudly vibrated. He looked at the screen, swiping to read a message, which he read aloud to the group. "It's Mary's dad. He says they are home safe, and the conversations have started."

Heather sighed. "That's good."

"There's more," Ron replied. "He says his wife accepts our gifts. He apologized for trying to push money on us. He says he has things to work on too, adding a smiley face." Ron looked knowingly at Heather. "You knew that would happen, didn't you?"

"I might have guessed," she laughed. "Men are so clueless sometimes."

Maura laughed, loudly adding "Hallelujah sister!".

The Montgomery children's faces all gaped in surprise; their mother's helper was usually so reserved.

"There's one last comment in the text," Ron said. "They are sitting down for a nice family dinner. Their family wishes us a merry Christmas and thanks us for everything we did today."

Heather held her hand to her heart.

Mark's stomach grumbled like a dump truck rumbling down a gravel road.

The room erupted in laughter.

Mark smiled broadly, patting his stomach. "I think we need to sit down to a nice family dinner too. I'm fading away over here."

Dale J. Moore

24 Around the Kitchen Table

The foursome sat around the kitchen table, eating their delectable Italian cuisine, enhanced with some lovely local red wine. Eating was only interrupted by sounds of enjoyment. Heather created a bevy of noises with each bite.

"Do you always moan like that when you eat?" Mark asked. "It's like you're recreating *When Harry Met Sally*. Not something a guy wants to hear from his sister."

Heather covered her mouth to snigger. She swallowed her food to respond. "Barry used to think it was cute. I think now he just tolerates it."

"I remember the sounds from when you were younger," Kevin added. "You've done that since you were a kid. You were just quieter about it back then."

"It was more an 'mmmm' noise back then," Mark stated. "More satisfaction than pleasure."

"At least," Heather commented, "I don't clear my throat during dinner. Remember how Dad made that guttural sound his last few years?"

"Yeah, that was gross," Ron grimaced. "I've always been an early riser. When I'd visit, he'd be hacking up a lung at five in the morning."

"I used to think it was due to him smoking those disgusting cigars," replied Kevin. "But I started doing it after dinner, before bed, and during the night. I'm afraid it's a hereditary thing. You guys will likely both get it soon enough," he smiled, looking at Mark, then Ron.

A look of total fear came over Ron. "Oh God help me if it does! That will drive me crazy."

"Not as much as it will drive Sharon nuts," chuckled Mark.

"That's for certain," Kevin sighed. "My throat clearing has Charlotte sending me to the spare room some nights."

"Aww," Heather pouted, reaching for the wine bottle to top up her glass. She passed the near empty bottle to Ron, who finished it. He got up to fetch a fresh bottle from the wine rack in the corner.

"It's part of getting old, you know. I turned fifty-eight this year." Kevin rolled his eyes skyward. "It gives you pause. Dad was only sixty-four when he died. That's only six years from now for me."

"And that's why," Mark said, "you are the math guy of the family. Ron would have come up with nine or ten, adding in his commission, fees, and assorted taxes, some made up. Like any sales guy worth his weight in add-ons would do."

Ron stood at the nearby kitchen island, maneuvering the corkscrew over the new wine bottle. With a low grunt he popped the cork. "At least I wouldn't have to measure it four times and write it down on a two-by-four, just to be sure."

Mark straightened up, laughing. He placed his fork down on his empty plate. "You got me on that one. Just following Dad's advice."

In unison they all quoted their father, "Measure twice and cut once, not the other way around!"

They all laughed heartily, tears coming to Heather's eyes from the joyful memories.

Mark took the new wine bottle from Ron. He poured himself a full glass, looking around the table at the mostly cleared plates. "Looks like everybody's done. How about we clear the table and retreat to the living room?"

"Sounds good," came replies around the table.

Kevin stood first, plate in hand. "I'll open another bottle of wine for you guys and bring it to the living room, so you don't run out as soon as you get comfortable."

Ron looked at his older brother. "You don't drink at all anymore, do you?"

Kevin nodded, looking toward the ground.

"Hey, I'm not criticizing at all, big brother. In fact, I'm proud you were able to lick your demons. I've known more guys than I can count that continue to struggle with addiction."

Kevin looked up, smiling. "Thanks, Ron. That means a lot to me."

Ron leaned closer. "Just don't tell anybody I said something nice to you. I've got an image to uphold, you know?"

"I promise not to tell," Kevin laughed.

Dale J. Moore

December 24th
Christmas Eve

25   The Living Room

The siblings settled into the comfortable couches in their mother's large living room. A pair of large Lazyboy recliners sat unoccupied at each end of the couches. A long coffee table glistened in front of the furniture, made from a meticulously sanded slab of wood, varnished to reveal an incredible grain. A large television hung mounted on the two-storey stone fireplace that adorned the centre of the back wall of the house. In the windows on either side of the fireplace, they could see large snowflakes tumbling to their resting place in the backyard. The wine began to flow freely. The conversation and laughing became raucous.

"What's your favourite 'Dad' story?" Heather asked Kevin.

"Easy one. Lions game, November 5, 1973. Against the Bears at Tiger Stadium. The Lions won the game. Greg Landry scored a touchdown. He was my favourite player back then. He had a brutal day otherwise, throwing four interceptions. I'd never seen that many people in one place. I was seven years old and Dad let me have three hot dogs."

"I bet you remember the troughs too," added Ron.

"Who could forget them?" Kevin replied.

"Troughs?" questioned Heather.

"Yes, the bathrooms had troughs along the floor against the walls where guys took a leak. No privacy and often too crowded for comfort," Ron replied.

"Eeew, gross!" Heather replied, repulsed by the mental image. "They don't have that anymore, do they?"

"The Joe had elevated troughs," Mark responded. "Very tight quarters, guys cramming in to release the beer they'd just had."

"Let's change the subject," Heather waved her arms in disgust. "What about you, Mark? Favourite Dad memory?"

"I'd have to say going to construction sites with him when I was ten or eleven years old," Mark said, straightening up to pour himself more wine.

Ron squirmed in his seat. Mark was unsure why Ron suddenly looked agitated. Mark continued. "Those were my favourite moments. I followed him around like a little sponge, soaking up as much information as possible." He paused to reflect, a grin appearing. "I think those were my favourite moments because I was too young for him to put to work. Once I turned twelve, he gave me jobs, which got more and more demanding – and tiring."

Ron shifted his weight, looking more restless by the moment.

Kevin didn't notice as he laughed at Mark's last comment. "We all took our turns being his gopher. You're right, it was fun until it became work. I remember watching Ron, then you, follow him around while I worked, thinking 'those were the days'." He sat back. "Of course, I was getting paid, and you guys weren't. There was some satisfaction there."

Mark looked at Kevin. "I remember when I found out you were getting paid, and how much it was. I couldn't wait until the next year."

"Do you remember coming to me in late July that summer?" Kevin asked Mark.

"I do. My friend Scott was moving out of town and I wanted to get him a going-away gift. It was a little fishing rod from the hardware store. I was a buck and change short. I asked you for a loan until my next allowance and you said no. I was devastated."

"And why did I say no?" Kevin asked.

"You don't loan money to family," Mark replied.

"Yep, Dad's number one rule," Kevin replied, sitting back.

Ron stood up suddenly, fuming. "Is that so? Too bad Dad didn't follow his own rules."

"What are you talking about?" Kevin asked.

Ron raised his voice, his arms moving frantically. "His loan to Mark. He lent money to Mark, but not to me!" He pointed at Mark. "He talked about not having favourites. Talk about two-faced."

Kevin approached Ron, trying to calm him down. Ron dismissed him with a back-handed swat. Ron added, "I hated him for that. I hated Mark for that." He looked at Heather. "You wanted favourite memories of Dad? Well, that was my least favourite." He picked up his glass and finished the wine inside. It looked for a second like he would throw the glass at the fireplace. His clenched fist stopped short of doing so.

Heather got off the couch, hoping to successfully mediate where Kevin had failed.

"There's some information that you don't have." She looked at Mark. "I'm not sure you even know the whole story."

Mark had sat quietly, feeling somewhat guilty about receiving the loan. "Mom just told me last week," he responded as he looked at Ron. "Look, I didn't know Dad had contributed to the loan. I thought it came from Mary, until last week."

Suddenly aware of his overly tight grasp on the wine glass, Ron set it gently on the table. "Does it matter? Dad knew."

Heather interrupted. "That's where you are wrong. I mean, he didn't know at the time of the loan. He thought he was giving the money to Mary as part of an investment group. She had misled Dad. It was one thing in her life that she felt truly bad about. She thought it was necessary to lie to Dad to keep Mark from going under."

"That's great," Ron sarcastically replied. "What about me? I was going under too. I had bills coming out of my ears that I couldn't pay. Neither her nor Dad lifted a finger to help me."

"You're right, they didn't. Yet you made your way through it didn't you?"

"Yes. It wasn't easy," Ron remarked.

"They both knew you would make it. You didn't have the other issues that Mark was facing, at least that's what Mary told me. She said choosing wasn't even that hard. Mary knew you would make it, no matter what. You had a kind of resilience that she envied."

"Really?" Ron said, now feeling embarrassed by his earlier outrage.

"Really," Heather smiled at her brother. "She knew Mark was coming from a dark place and needed help getting out from there. You didn't need the help. In fact, she said you'd be better off not getting help. It would make you stronger."

Ron looked at Mark. "I'm sorry for holding a grudge about the loan for so long. Especially with this new information. I feel stupid now."

"You and me both. Hatchet buried?" Mark reached out to shake hands.

"Agreed," Ron nodded. "Sorry, man."

Mark looked at him as they shook hands. "What about that hit into the boards?"

Ron laughed. "I don't say sorry to anyone, except Sharon. So twice in one day ain't going to happen."

"Good enough," Mark grinned back.

Having fetched another bottle of wine along with some snacks, the family regrouped.

"Okay, I think we covered Dad moments pretty good." Kevin looked around the room. "Now that everyone has made up and we are all cheerful again, I think we should do a family roast. You know, all in good fun. I'll start with Real Estate Ron since he's now in a forgiving mood."

"All right, let me have it," Ron motioned with his hand to his oldest brother. "Bring it on."

Kevin stood up in the centre of the room. "Here's Ron, schmoozing one of his clients." He wet his hand from his glass of water, slicking back his hair to mock his brother. He sucked in his slight gut, pulling his shoulders back and up. "Let's imagine Ron talking to a young successful couple." He put his arm around an imaginary client. "He approaches the man first," he said, clearing his throat. He talked in a deep manly voice. "This condo just screams your name. You're an engineer, right? You can see the quality of the workmanship here. Everything is solid. The best engineers designed this tower. It's a freaking work of art. The amount of steel in here is mahoosive. I think it's rated for a magnitude nine hundred earthquake and thousand metre tidal surge."

Heather blurted out a laugh. "Ah, yes. Those Lake Ontario tidal surges we all fear."

Kevin broke character to grin, then resumed his real-estate Ron impression. "I know engineers like you work very hard for your money. Let me say this, you are getting an exceptional deal by becoming one of the first customers in this tower. You'll impress your wife with the deal you're getting here. She'll think you are 'the man'."

Kevin stopped, switching arms to embrace another imaginary person. "Now his wife," he cleared his throat again. He began talking in a soft, understanding voice. "Am I wrong, or does this palace ooze class, like you? Look at the view! Can you picture yourself cozied up on the couch with a great book, the horizon filled by Lake Ontario? Magnificent." Kevin flashed an oversized smile. "What? The burned-out building across the street? Oh no, they're removing that next week. A store that sells rainbows, butterflies, and unicorns is taking its place." He paused again. "No, absolutely not. That's not the foundation of a taller building going up right in front of the window here. Your lake view is guaranteed, at least until you move in, provided it's in the next sixty days."

Even Ron laughed at the imitation.

Mark jumped up. "Let me in on this." He slapped five with Kevin as his brother sat down. "Okay, this is Ron closing the deal," he coughed, trying to pose like Kevin had. "I'm not going to waste wine slicking back my hair."

His sister laughed.

Mark started his impersonation. "Okay, Mr. and Mrs. Engineer, I've got your paperwork for you. I've checked with the builder. Through intense negotiations, I've managed to get an extra one hundred and forty two dollars and twelve cents off your purchase price, leaving the cost well below four million dollars. Well, one hundred and forty two-plus dollars below. Your combined income puts you just below the financial approval line but, and I stress I don't do this for everybody, I burned a few favours. I got you a loan, albeit with a slightly," he pinched his fingers together, "higher interest rate." He pretended to look at his clients. "How much more? Oh, just a measly seven percent above the normal rate – and that's after I reduced my cut to five percent of that seven percent. I'm practically taking a loss here."

"There's that Ron math again," laughed Kevin.

Mark continued. "Oh, I forgot the best news! I got the builder to throw in an extra peephole on your front door. One at the height of each of you. No stooping or standing on tiptoe. Isn't that amazing?"

Ron burst out laughing. "Have you got a spy cam on me? I think I did that deal last week." He stood up to pat his brother on the back. "Although I must admit that extra peephole is a new upsell for me. Have you added that to your custom builds, Mark?"

"No, just thought of it."

"Alright, my turn for payback," Ron said. He glanced around the room. "As much as I should get revenge on Kevin, I'm going to go with Mark." Ron stood up, sticking his gut out, what little there was. "Now howdy there, Tex" — he shook hands with an imaginary man — "and ma'am. I'm happier than a pig in shit that you all have come to my model house here to have a gander."

"Like I talk like that," Mark laughed.

"Alberta is the Texas of Canada," Kevin replied.

Ron continued. "Let's start in the basement. As you know, a house is like a marriage. It needs a strong foundation. Am I right? Am I right? Of course, I'm right. I'm Mark the Builder." Ron laughed at himself. He pointed upwards. "Now you can see here the supports for the main floor. We save ourselves money, I mean we save you money, by skirting that government rule of using two-by-ten lumber or steel braces by using a bunch of secondhand two-by-fours, fastened securely together with a staple gun. You'll notice we use double staples as a quality measure – at no extra cost to you. It also means I can use untrained high school kids trying to earn their community hours to do the work, saving more money. Mostly for me, but I pass a few bucks down to you."

"You make it sound like using child labour is a bad thing?" Mark replied, deadpan.

"Right, eh?" Ron replied. "Builds character in them." He paused to take a long drink of wine. "Okay, I've got a bit more."

"You've always boasted that," Kevin chimed in.

Ron laughed. "Don't you know it. Continuing with my skit …if you look down, your basement has a high quality gravel floor. The kids,

I mean labourers, rake it five times – did you all hear me? FIVE times!" he held up his hand to show four fingers. He looked at his hand, then popped out the thumb to show five. "Five. You know what I find annoying in other new builds? Hm? I'll tell you. Cracks. Cracks in the basement floor. How ugly is that? No cracks in a 'Mark the Builder' basement floor, no siree! Just smooth gravel." With the others laughing, Ron took a bow.

"Heather? Do you want to take on Kevin?"

"I have a few things to say to my financial planner brother, but I'm just going to stay sitting."

"Too much wine, sis?" Mark asked.

"Is there such a thing as too much wine, Mark? Is there?" she glared at him, then laughed. "As far as Kev goes, I think it's very brave for him to risk other people's money, instead of his own. I mean, there is no risk for him – he gets his commission if the client loses money! Better still, he gets even more if they make money. How do you beat that gig?"

Kevin nodded. "Guilty as charged."

"I'm just going to tell you," Heather replied, "that you have become a nicer person since you left that stock market job. Or maybe it's Charlotte's influence."

"Hey!"

Ron jumped in. "You're supposed to trash him, not boost him up. You never were very good at this game."

"I guess not," Heather smiled. "But as they say, people in glass houses…"

"With that," Kevin started, "my turn to talk about Heather." He stood up. "I'm not going to try to impersonate her. My voice is way too deep to impersonate a woman."

"Yes, and you also make an ugly woman," Mark stated. "We have proof, if you remember."

Kevin chuckled.

"You played the red-headed girl in your class re-enactment of *Charlie Brown's Christmas*," Mark laughed. "Red wig and all. Funny, but fugly."

"How could I forget? I had the nickname 'Red' for the rest of the year. I had brown hair." Kevin cracked a partial smile. "So Heather, what can I say? Do you even own a house out there in B.C., or do you live in an environmentally friendly mud hut? I was surprised when you said Barry had an F-150 – I thought he'd have a dogsled or something that doesn't pollute, except what they leave on the ground of course." He lifted his shoe, giving a disgusted look at the sole. "By the way, when you drove the car – I could barely tell that you hadn't driven in ten or more years." He cupped his hands over his face, peeked between his fingers, then repeated it, cringing his body. "I guess it's not like riding a bike after all."

"Who says she could ride a bike?" Ron interrupted.

"Oh yeah, I forgot about that," Mark said. "What was that, Heather? Grade six. No wait, I was in grade six. You were in grade five."

"Yep, grade five. Three weeks ahead of summer vacation. I was riding the hand-me-down bike from Mary. She was driving by then and had little use for a bike. I loved that bike," she sighed. "But it was trashed after that."

"You were trashed after that too!" Mark replied. "I've never seen a leg bend like that when we came to get you."

"That's because they don't bend like that," Heather answered. "They break. I must have ridden those hills around the new subdivision a hundred times. I remember we were racing. I think there were three of us. I took the lead. I came flying over a hill and it wasn't until I was in mid-air that I spotted the portable cement mixer. If you don't know this," she laughed again, "it's impossible to change direction on a bike once you are airborne. I was able to tip the bike back, but my leg slammed into the steel mixer. Fortunately, I had built up such a lead in the race that the other girls didn't come barrelling down on me too."

"Ruined much of that summer for you, didn't it?"

"I got good at puzzles," she grinned. "And spent a lot of time with Mom watching movies."

"There's a segue if I ever heard one," Kevin said. "How about we throw on a Christmas movie?"

Dale J. Moore

December 24th
Christmas Eve

26   Memories

It was after ten o'clock when the movie *Elf* finished. Most of them shouted out familiar dialogue throughout the movie. Kevin had brought with him a green and gold elf hat that adorned his head the whole movie, except for the five times that Mark flipped it off his head from behind. A debate raged on for ten minutes about what movie to watch next. Finally, Heather got up.

"I'm going outside to smoke a joint. I'm happy with whatever you guys decide to watch." Slipping on her boots, she pulled on her coat on the way out the back door. 'A Christmas Eve with snow in Windsor', she said to herself. 'What do you know? Miracles do happen.' She walked around the backyard, following a flagstone path to a gazebo near the back of the yard. She turned to look back at the house, taking a long drag as she did. Large flakes landed and melted on her head. She looked up to watch the snow fall, a flake landing in her eye, triggering a blink. The cloudy sky covered the few stars that were usually visible from this area. A plethora of stars littered the night sky at home – her home. Less artificial lighting and industry eliminated most of the light pollution. When she'd first moved out there, she was truly in awe. It felt like stepping onto a different planet – in more ways than the stars. She suffered lifestyle shock for the first six months, then loneliness for the next year. Until she met Barry. She'd always had a soft spot for environmental issues and saving the planet causes but had never lived in a place that exhibited the best of what needed saving. Toronto didn't need saving – well, maybe from itself at times she thought.

She shook her head, her naturally greying brown hair shedding the now accumulating flakes. The joint had burned down to her fingertips. She had one last pull on it, dropping it to the flagstone to snuff out with her foot. She bent down to scoop up the evidence only to notice the uneven ground beside her where the stump had lingered. She thought the yard looked different from her memory. Initially, she discounted it to the dark and bleakness of winter. What remained of the stump had been removed prior to her last trip. She had forgotten, possibly due to the brevity of her prior visit. Then she had a terrible flashback about Mary.

Mary became pregnant late in grade thirteen, the last year of high school in those days. Danny Miller, one of the school jocks, did the honourable thing and they were married at summer's end. They seemed reasonably happy despite their meagre incomes and the huge lifestyle adjustment for Mary when they moved into a small one bedroom apartment. Danny had started a job selling cars in his father's used car lot. It couldn't have paid much back then. Heather knew Mom had to have helped Mary out financially to even afford what they had. Mary had taken a couple of part-time jobs once little Christopher was old enough for day care. Christopher had inherited his father's athleticism, obviously better than kids a year or two older in any sport he tried. At Christopher's sixth birthday party in mid-September, Mom had Mary's family over for lunch and presents. It was a warm day and festivities took place in the backyard, along with the annual swatting of yellowjackets. After eating, blowing out candles, and opening gifts, they settled in to enjoy the sun before cool fall weather settled in. Danny and Christopher played catch with a football while Mary chatted with her parents. As with any six-year-old, Christopher soon tired of his current game and sought his next adventure. He ran off to climb his favourite tree in Grandma's backyard. Danny grabbed a fresh beer and joined the other adults. Mary asked Danny where their son had gone. He pointed up to the tree. Mary yelled up to Christopher to not climb so high, but Danny encouraged his son to go higher. It happened so fast that nobody could do anything. Christopher stepped on a weak branch, losing his grip on the one above him. Gravity took control from there, sending the boy hurtling back to earth, hitting his head hard on the flagstone path that led to the pool house. Mary shoved her husband aside to bolt toward her still son. Her mom called 911. Christopher had perished immediately.

Mary was grief-stricken, unable to function for weeks. Danny looked for someone to blame, driving a spike between them. In his mind, Mary should have watched Christopher closer: she should have stood firm and told Danny to not let his son climb higher; Mary's parents should have pruned the weak branches, etc.

Not able to look at Mary, and her not responsive to his needs, Danny sought solace in the arms of other women. Many other women. A different one every night from whatever bar he'd wandered into that day after work. Alcohol became his coping mechanism. It failed him

163

miserably. Danny finally lost it on a weekend in early October. He'd been drinking all morning, got in the latest car his father had loaned him, and drove to the Montgomery household. Parking the used car haphazardly with one set of wheels on the lawn beside the wide driveway, he opened the trunk to pull out a gas-powered chain saw. He staggered through the side gate, stopping on the inside to fire up the chain saw. Determination burning in his eyes, he made straight for the tree that killed his son. He began hacking away at the tree trunk, not knowing what he was doing and much too drunk to be doing it anyway. As Mr. Montgomery came running to the backyard, the tree trunk buckled. Danny moved around the tree to finish it off. Mr. Montgomery yelled fruitlessly, his voice obscured by the roaring saw. The tree came down quicker than Danny could have imagined. The large maple crashed violently, taking out part of the pool house as it struck a very startled Danny. Christopher's father almost didn't survive the ambulance ride to the hospital, narrowly avoiding becoming the second victim of the tree.

In a matter of weeks, Mary's life had been thrown upside down. The chain saw episode was the final straw with Danny. She knew about his indiscretions but had been too lost in grief to do anything about them until then. She left Danny, not so much repulsed by the ugly scar from his eye to his ear and the gash on the back of his head from the falling tree, but by his behaviour since Christopher's accident. She moved back in with her parents. The stump in the backyard lay as a constant reminder of her pain. She moved to Toronto to start fresh.

December 24th
Christmas Eve

27   Movie Time

Heather approached the back door, looking inside to see her three brothers enjoying themselves on the couch. *Must be another comedy*, she thought. Approaching the back door, she stomped her feet, shook her head again, and brushed down her coat of the white stuff. She entered to the sound of the Drifters' version of "White Christmas". As she closed the door, the boys let out a loud 'ARRRR' scream. Kevin in *Home Alone* had just slapped his face with aftershave.

"Can you grab another bottle of red?" Mark hollered to his sister.

She draped her coat over the kitchen chair after neatly placing her boots on the mat. Corkscrew successfully employed, she carried the open bottle to the living room, along with a few bags of snacks.

"Junk food!" Ron roared approval. "What have you got?"

Heather held up each bag and tossed them one by one to the boys, keeping a handful of Swedish berries obscured safely from others in her pocket.

After calling each other 'you filthy animal' repeatedly for five minutes, the movie in front of them had progressed into the slapstick sections, reminding them of real-life incidents.

"Hey, Mark," Ron laughed, "I'm sure you remember practising to sneak down the stairs to see Santa."

"How could I forget your sabotage."

"Come on, nobody got hurt … except your pride, perhaps," Ron added.

"Do you remember that, Heather?" Kevin asked. "You were pretty young."

"I remember you guys teasing Mark for a few years after. I don't really remember the details," she replied.

Kevin continued. "Every year we practised sneaking down the stairs, just before Christmas, on a night Mom and Dad were at some party. Usually Mary was the ringleader, but she had a party at the neighbours the same night. That left me in charge." Kevin paused to take a drink. "We laid out pillows and blankets on all the stairs to silence the squeaky hardwood steps. We had you go first, since you were the lightest. If you caused any stair to make noise, we'd fix it before the bigger kids came down. Ron waited at the bottom to greet you, after you'd practised peering through the railings at the fireplace to check for the fat man."

Ron chimed in. "No, not Kevin. That was before he added those pounds."

"Thanks for that," Kevin sneered. "Anyway, we convinced Mark that it would be very dark on Christmas Eve and that he should practise with a blindfold. At the top of the stairs, I put Mary's pink frilly sleeping mask on him and had him put his hand on the railing for balance."

Ron jumped in. "Meanwhile, I replaced the pillows on the last two steps with water balloons. We spread out Lego blocks on the foyer landing."

Kevin took over. "Ron nodded that he was ready, and I got Mark to slowly move down the stairs. As he got near the end, 'bang' the first water balloon soaked his foot. Startled, he stepped down again, saturating his other foot. He tugged his mask off as he took the final step, right onto the painful blocks. He screamed as loudly as Ron and I laughed."

"Yeah, it was flipping hilarious," Mark replied. "And Heather, while these clowns were laughing, you came over to see if I was okay."

Heather smiled.

"But I got the last laugh. They told me to clean up the watery mess before it stained the wood and Mom gave me heck. They said they'd blame it on me. I told them no," he pointed at his foot, "I said I had the marks on my feet to prove they'd caused it." He grinned. "They used about ten towels to wipe it all up. It was fun to watch."

"I have to admit, little brother," Ron grinned back. "You grew some backbone that day. I didn't mind cleaning it up because you finally stood up to our crap."

"I'd say," said Kevin. "I remember a few years later, Mark got us back pretty good."

"The toboggan incident," laughed Ron. "He certainly pulled one over us that year."

Mark leaned back, pleased with himself. "That was a good one." He looked at his sister. "You'd gone Christmas shopping with Mom and Mary. We had fresh snow the night before. We were totally wired to get the toboggan and sled out and hit the hill. Dad gave us a lift, saying he'd come back in two hours to get us. We trekked to the top of the hill, them carrying the toboggan and me the blue plastic sled. I knew they'd want the toboggan as it could get up good speed with the two of them riding together."

"It was a beautiful sunny day, if I remember," Kevin added. "The sun caused a bit of glare on the hill making it hard to see too far in front of you as you descended."

"It was indeed sunny," Mark replied. "You guys let me go first, to get a feel for the path downhill. I had a good ride and popped up with my sled to get out of the way."

"Safety first," Heather laughed.

"The boys came down right behind me, though a little to the left. Ron made some remark to Kevin about steering harder to the right next time. We grabbed our rides and clambered back up the hill. This time, they pushed me out of the way, saying they were going first. I stepped back and watched, hoping this run would do it."

"And it did," Kevin moaned, holding his back.

Mark chuckled. "They got positioned on the toboggan and asked me to give them a push to get a better start. I pushed as hard as I could. They took off fast down the hill. Right after they started, I heard Ron yelling at Kevin 'Pull right!' Kevin yanked the rope hard. The steering board at the front of the toboggan came off in his hands, flying over his head and clipping Ron in the noggin. Terrified, they were helpless as the toboggan veered hard right, off the side of the hill and into some waiting evergreen trees. I swear, I almost pissed my pants laughing. Until I realized they might be hurt. I jumped on my plastic sled toward where they went airborne. I got there and these two knuckleheads were laughing their heads off, saying that was the most awesome ride ever!"

"We didn't know he'd tampered with the sled," Kevin remembered, "until Dad picked us up and he surveyed the damage. He could tell someone had loosened the bolts because nothing snapped."

"Fortunately, Dad was there to protect me when they found out." Mark added. "Dad laughed about it, telling them that he didn't want to see any revenge on their part. He told them they'd caused me enough grief over the past few years."

"Yeah, we had to wait a whole year to get revenge," Ron said, rubbing his hands together, "didn't we, Kevin?"

"It hardly seems fair that you two oldest boys picked on the youngest!" protested Heather.

"Survival of the fittest, and all that," Ron replied.

"We were just toughening him up," Kevin added.

"Like Kevin in *Home Alone*," Ron said. "The first movie toughened him up so he could handle the bad guys without the home field advantage in the second movie."

Dale J. Moore

December 25th
Christmas Day (Barely)

28 *Discovery*

At midnight, the group decided something more substantial than chips was needed due to the amount they'd drunk already. A fridge raid uncovered leftover pizza and the remains of the three boxes of Kraft Dinner that Kevin had made for lunch. They seamlessly resumed a decades-old argument over whether leftover pizza was best reheated or cold, resulting in an evenly split vote. All but Ron preferred the KD cold. They stood around the kitchen island, devouring the remnants of the prior meals.

"Cold pizza is so gross," Mark commented, readying to bite into his heated square. A mushroom and stick of pepperoni slid off his pizza.

Heather laughed. "That's why you eat it cold. The cheese is congealed and holds the toppings in place." She turned her pizza upside down to prove her point, only to have a piece of green pepper tumble to the marble countertop below.

"Yep," Mark chuckled. "You sure made your point on that one."

"Well," Ron stated, "there is no contesting that my cold Kraft Dinner sticks together better than the hot stuff."

"Yeah, but that's just gross," Heather cringed.

"No way," Ron countered. "Putting that big lump of noodles into my mouth all at once is heaven!"

"I still say it's gross," Heather replied, face scrunched up.

Finishing their snack, Heather wiped down their paper plates and tossed them into the recycle bin. Kevin collected the cheesy bowls, giving them a quick rinse.

"You guys up for another movie?" Mark asked.

Ron checked his watch. "Getting kind of late for me."

Heather gave her brother the pouty look.

"Okay, okay," Ron replied, hands up in surrender. "I'll watch the first part anyway."

Heather grinned, rubbing his arm in approval.

Mark rattled off movie titles, with the group settling on *White Christmas*.

While Mark hunted for the movie on the streaming services, Kevin stood close to the tree, admiring the decorations. Heather joined him.

"Remember when we made these paper train ornaments?" Kevin asked his sister. A set of five train cars hung in a row, connected with string. Each car had a name across the middle, with cotton balls making pretend smoke out of the engine and snow at the wheels.

"I remember doing lots of crafts with Mom." She gently touched the engine, her finger tracing the spelling of Mary's name. The middle cars had the boys' names in age order, with the caboose carrying her name.

"I'm surprised it's held up all this time," Kevin stated. "It's been what, over forty years? It's hard to fathom that it's been that long."

"None of us are kids anymore," Heather sighed. "Heck, your kids aren't kids anymore. Their kids are kids!" She laughed.

"Sad but true," Kevin said, bending down to look at other ornaments. "What's this?" he asked, reaching for an envelope near the back of the tree. "It's sealed. Says 'My Family' on the front and 'X-mas 2014' on the back." He flipped it back to the front. "This doesn't look like Mom's writing." He pointed at the front. "Is that your writing?"

"No," Heather said, covering her mouth in shock. "It's Mary's."

"That's odd." Kevin puzzled over the envelope, flipping it over a few times. "Mary passed away in 2013. I wonder why Mom didn't open it the next year. That's clearly when Mary wanted it opened."

He handed it to Heather.

"It's not addressed just to her, that's why. It's addressed to the family."

Mark paused the movie. He and Ron stood up to examine the mystery in Heather's hands.

"Mom was probably waiting," Ron speculated.

"For what?" Kevin asked.

"For all of us to get together. Mary likely figured we'd continue to gather for the holidays. Mom probably didn't want to open it without us."

"But she never even mentioned it," Mark pointed out.

173

"Knowing Mom," Heather commented, "she figured it would happen when it happened, and she didn't want to force the issue."

"So do we open it?" Ron asked, looking around at his siblings.

"Why not?" Ron asked. "We're all here."

"We're not all here," Kevin quickly pointed out. "Mom is in the hospital."

"Kevin's right, we should take it up to Mom's room tomorrow and open it then."

Mark nodded in agreement.

Ron nervously rocked back and forth. "I think it will drive me crazy waiting. You know how this kind of thing is a trigger for me."

"I thought you were 'medicated' enough by now that it wouldn't bother you," Heather said.

"You'd think …" Ron forced a twitchy grin. "You know, Kevin is sober. He can drive us down there."

Kevin took a deep breath. "In case you didn't notice, it is *way* past visiting hours."

A devious look crossed Ron's face. "What if we weren't visitors."

Heather laughed. "What? Are you going to dress up as Doctor Inebriated?"

"No, of course not," Ron replied. "Transport personnel. You know, the crew that moves patients between hospitals or to nursing homes, or wherever."

"What's the plan? You're going to steal some uniforms and waltz in there?" Kevin chuckled.

Ron stared at him. "Don't be ridiculous. My buddy Tom from high school runs a patient transport company. He owes me one. I'm going to call him."

Mark looked at his watch. "At this time? It must be a big favour that he owes you."

"You don't want to know," Ron replied, eyes wide. Pulling out his phone he walked away with the device beside his ear.

Heather watched him leave. "Is it me, or has Ron gone off the deep end on this one?"

"I don't know," Mark responded. "If we wait until morning, it likely means I won't sleep all night worrying about the letter."

Kevin nodded. "As much as I think Ron has a problem, I have to agree with Mark. I won't sleep a wink." He put up his hands, palms forward. "Not that I condone this idea."

Ron strode back into the living room, sliding his phone into his back pocket. "Tom will arrive here at five forty-five in the morning to pick us up. It's the earliest I could get him to do. He says it won't raise suspicion at that time and they will have limited staff on the holiday. Should reduce questions and problems."

"What are normal visiting hours?" Mark asked.

"Not until ten in the morning," Heather replied.

Kevin nodded agreement. "We get to know four hours earlier what's in the letter. I guess it's worth it. I'm off to bed."

175

Dale J. Moore

December 25th
Christmas Morning

29 Transporters

At five thirty in the morning, Maura arrived at the Montgomery household. She was surprised to find the front door unlocked and planned to remind Lizzie's kids that LaSalle wasn't as burglar-free as it was twenty years earlier – especially at Christmas. Opening the door, she dropped her bag at the sight of the four grown children sitting around the living room with their coats on.

"Maura," a surprised Heather said. "We thought you were asleep in your room."

"I spent Christmas Eve at my cousin's place, with her kids."

"Nice visit?" Kevin asked.

Maura nodded.

"You didn't need to come back so early," Ron stated.

"Your mother asked me to make Christmas dinner," Maura bluntly replied. "I'm here to start preparations."

"You know that she won't make it home for dinner, don't you?" Mark asked, sure she knew his mother's condition wouldn't improve overnight to that point.

"Of course. Your mother would want me to cook a full dinner with all the sides. She'd likely fire me if I didn't feed you Christmas dinner," she frowned, looking down to the ground.

"I thought you already quit?" Ron asked.

"I gave my two weeks' notice. I intend to work as normal until that time is up."

"Okay," Heather smiled. "I'm sure dinner will be amazing."

"Where are you going so early?" Maura inquired.

"The hospital," they responded in staggered unison.

"Oh dear," Maura replied. "I should have told you visiting hours aren't until ten this morning."

"We know," Ron assured her. "I've made arrangements to see her earlier."

A loud knock came from the wooden front doors.

"And there's our ride now," Ron told her. "We'll get back in a few hours."

"Thanks," Maura replied, turning to look at Heather. "Would you mind keeping an eye on the turkey later when I head down to visit your mother?"

"Sure," Heather replied, placing a hand gently on Maura's arm. "When we get back you can give us instructions."

The foursome got into the back of Tom's transport vehicle, the guys helping each other to put on the uniforms in the crammed space. By the time they arrived at the hospital, Tom had laid out the plan of what they needed to do to look official and not get him in any real trouble. Heather would play the daughter with power of attorney. The guys were Tom's crew.

Tom parked the truck in the loading zone, per normal process. Exiting the elevator on their mother's floor, Tom took a clipboard with documents to the nurses' station. The nurse barely glanced at the paperwork, with Tom a familiar friendly face who'd chatted her up several times.

"London, eh?" the nurse said as she skimmed the papers. "Tough for you on Christmas Day."

"It is what it is," Ron shrugged. "At least I got through Christmas Eve uninterrupted."

She put the clipboard on the counter in front of her.

Tom nodded at the others. Ron and Kevin pushed the gurney toward their mother's room.

The nurse spotted Heather. "I'm sorry, miss. Visiting hours don't start until ten."

Tom stepped forward, putting on an apologetic face. "I'm sorry," he glanced at her name tag to be sure, "Nancy. She's the daughter and will travel with us to London."

"Tom, you know procedure. She can't go in the room with you. She can wait out here with me, okay?"

Tom nodded. "Of course, Nancy. Guess I'm still tired from Christmas Eve. Long night putting together playsets for the grandkids."

The nurse grinned back. "At least bikes come pre-assembled these days."

Heather remained as the others rolled on to the room.

"Jesus, Ron," Tom exclaimed, seeing Mrs. Montgomery's bandaged head and hands. "I'm sorry. I didn't realize she was this bad."

"No problem, Ron. I'm sure you deal with these situations a lot."

"Yeah, but it's harder when it's someone you know. I remember your mom making us soup and sandwiches after we spent all morning on your backyard rink."

Ron nodded. "Tell us how we load her onto the gurney. You said we should take her down to the lobby to read the letter. Then we'll bring her right back."

Tom guided them through the steps. To his relief, the sons got their mother on the gurney without dropping her, damaging her bandaging, or ripping her intravenous tube from her arm. Tom strapped the patient down, though there was no way she was going anywhere based on the vitals check he'd performed.

Kevin and Ron carefully guided the gurney out of the room, pausing at the nurses' station for a final signature from nurse Nancy. Tom bid adieu and the group, including Heather, targeted the elevator. Once the doors closed, they let out a collective sigh of relief.

"You boys did good," Tom grinned. Laughing, he added, "I'll give you a call if any of my crew gets Christmas flu in the next few days."

"No thanks," Kevin replied. "I'm too old for this shit. I thought my heart was going to explode from anxiety."

The elevator door opened to a waiting Mark. "I found a room around the corner we can use to read the letter."

"Sorry, we can't do that," Tom objected. "I can't explain if I'm found in a room with a patient." He looked around at the others. "We'll have to take her to the truck. You can have privacy there and I can follow my normal procedure. It won't look suspicious."

"Won't it look odd sitting in the loading zone?" Mark asked.

"I'll just take us for a short drive and come back," Tom replied. They nodded.

Arriving at the truck, Tom instructed and aided his new crew on how to load and lock their mother's gurney in place for safe transport. They took spots on the benches along both sides.

Heather pulled out the letter. "Ready, boys?"

They nodded approval.

"Okay, here goes." She looked at her mother. "Mom, I'm opening the letter that Mary left, that you've been keeping on the tree all these years." She paused as if waiting for a response, though none was expected. She cleared her throat, proceeding to slip a finger under the fold of the envelope. Heather carefully slipped the folded letter from its decade-old resting place. She flattened out the two pages to begin reading.

"'Dear family, I'm so happy that you have kept the Montgomery Christmas tradition alive!'" Heather choked up, looking guiltily around at her brothers. They shared a look of failure. Heather continued. "'Christmas has no doubt been difficult on Mom, having lost our father and now me close to the holiday season. I'm glad she's had all of you to lean on.'" Heather paused to wipe tears and dig for a tissue from her pocket. She held the letter out to Kevin. He took the pages, scanning down to the point in the letter his sister had stopped. He coughed then read:

"'I hope you were able to bring your kids too. There's nothing like children to bring the house to life for her favourite holiday.'" Kevin looked around, another failure. He continued. "'So now for the surprise! I bought you each a gift, a small attempt to say thank you for all you've done for me over the years. I left them in a box in my room. Hopefully Mom didn't donate it yet (you know how she hates clutter).'"

"Ain't that the truth," Mark confirmed.

Kevin read some more. "'Anyway, I hope you enjoy the gifts. To paraphrase my favourite Christmas movie, 'There's room for all of you on the nice list' – Merry Christmas!'"

Silence filled the back of the truck, each sibling lost for words as they searched each other for something to say. Finally, Ron broke the quiet.

"We have to take her home," he said flatly.

"What?!" exclaimed Kevin. "Are you crazy?"

"We can't take her home," echoed Heather.

"No ... no, Ron has a point," countered Mark, again on the same page as Ron. He turned to face the front and hollered up to Tom at the wheel. "How long before someone checks to see if the patient arrived in London?"

"Two hours or more."

"Take us home please. All of us," Mark replied, assuring his siblings with a nod.

December 25th
Christmas Morning

30   Home for Christmas

Kevin opened wide both wooden front doors of the house to allow his mother's gurney to pass through, guided by Ron and Mark on each side. Tom supervised from the head of the bed.

Maura dropped the dishcloth from her hand at the sight of her employer entering the home. She whispered some Portuguese, making the cross to bless Lizzie's entrance to the home.

"What have you done?" Maura asked.

"It's a long story," Ron answered.

"Did Mom have you put presents from Mary under the tree?" Kevin asked excitedly.

"No. And she didn't put any under the tree by herself. The only presents are the ones that I brought yesterday. Your mother never put her presents out until Christmas morning."

"They must be in Mary's room still," Kevin suggested.

"Nobody's been in Mary's room for years," Heather cautioned.

"We don't have a choice, do we?" Ron said, shrugging his shoulders.

They carefully rolled their mother close to the Christmas tree, asking Maura to watch her. Not that their mother was going anywhere. They just felt better that somebody stay with her.

With Heather in the lead, they filed down the hallway. She cautiously took hold of the door handle, pausing to look at her brothers for the go-ahead. With nods all around, she slowly turned the handle and pushed the door open. For her, it felt like going back ten years through a time machine. Aside from a generous dose of dust, it remained as Heather remembered it. Her heart sank as she spotted a picture of Mary cuddling with her son Christopher. Hardcover copies of her novels stood at one end of the dresser, Mary's smile gleaming from the back cover of the last one in the row, a reminder of happier times. With clutter on the floor and chair, it was obvious their mother had not stepped foot in the room since Mary's passing. Either that or she simply couldn't bear to touch anything, afraid of shattering a memory by moving something.

Kevin sneezed, shattering the silence of dread.

"Sorry," he apologized. He sneezed again onto his sleeve. "All the dust."

"She said they are in a box," Ron stated. "I'll check the closet. Mark, can you look under the bed?"

"I'll check the dresser," Heather volunteered.

"I'll just stay out in the hallway," Kevin said, quickly followed by another sneeze and a quietly spoken 'sorry'.

It didn't take Ron long to call out that he'd found something. Heather closed the dresser drawer she'd been rummaging through. Mark got up off the floor.

"Dude," Ron laughed at Mark. "You look like you've aged ten years."

Heather and Kevin looked, also laughing.

Mark glanced in the wall mirror. A thick layer of dust from under the bed covered his head, completely greying his hair. He swiped at his hair, sending a plume of dust into the air.

Kevin sneezed again. Covering his face, he moved out of the doorway and into the fresh hallway air.

Ron moved the box to the bed, lifting the top to reveal cards and presents. "Yep, this is it." He placed the lid back on top. "Let's get it downstairs and go through it."

From the hallway came a request from Kevin. "Can you dust the box first, please?"

Ron yanked a tissue from a nearby box, only to see the dust collected on it scatter through the air. He grabbed a few more tissues, ones that had kept clean under the plastic seal on the box. He wiped the box, then glanced down at his shirt. Transporting the box had left a grey residue. He wiped that down too.

"Are you done yet," Mark joked.

"No, I think I missed a spot," Ron replied, quickly swiping his hand off the side of Mark's head.

"Guess I deserved that," Mark laughed.

Gathering around the Christmas tree, the group stared at the open box, lid propped against the side. Maura placed a charcuterie board in the center of the coffee table, with some small plates and dessert forks.

"Do you mind if I stay?" Maura asked.

"Not at all," Heather replied before one of her brothers could respond to the contrary.

Maura smiled, happy to feel welcomed. She sat down to the side, near her friend Lizzie.

The children agreed they would proceed youngest to oldest, an order they'd adopted playing board games all those years ago.

Heather reached into the box and pulled out her card. She flipped it over, grinning at the back.

"What is it?" Kevin asked.

"It says 'made from one hundred percent recycled paper'. That's Mary. Thinking about the little things that would make me happy."

She opened the envelope, pulling out a card with a right jolly old Santa. She showed it to the others. Another envelope fell from inside the card. She fetched it from the floor, setting it on the table in front of her. She read the card. 'Dear Heather, Merry Christmas to my favourite sister. We've always been peas in a pod about the environment, so I thought you'd appreciate what's in the envelope. Early last year (2013), I bought two hundred shares in a new company that is promising to build affordable electric cars. I saw the shares had gone up this fall. By the time you open this, the stock may not be worth the paper it's printed on. Even if that's true, at least you invested five hundred dollars in a green future. I hope that puts a smile on your face.'" Heather paused to dab a tissue on a fresh tear. She picked up the second envelope and carefully opened it. She held it up. "It's two hundred original shares in Tesla."

"That will pay a few bills," Ron stated. "Those are worth a pretty penny now."

Heather searched the box to retrieve her gift. It had a large tag on the front that she read aloud. "'I hope you get a kick out of this. Just a small reminder of our time together.'" Heather tore off the wrapping paper to reveal a five-by-seven picture frame.

"What's it a picture of?" Kevin queried.

"It's Mary and I celebrating with cocktails. She had someone take this with her camera when we visited the restaurant before her rendezvous with Jeff. I guess she scouted the restaurant as the perfect place to get that jerk of an ex-boyfriend of mine arrested. Mom only recently told me that Mary had orchestrated the entire exit of my ex." She laughed. "It was brilliant. She was brilliant."

Kevin put his arm around his sister.

"My turn." Mark stood up to approach the box. He plucked out his card and gift, which also looked like a picture frame.

"Okay, here goes." Mark opened the card and read from inside of the wintery farmhouse scene. "'You were a great baby brother. I know you took it on the chin a lot from the older boys, but you endured. I'm so proud that you were able to defeat your demons. I know you made Dad proud that you saved your business and that he saw you turn it around into a thriving enterprise. I know you and Patty like taking the kids to Florida in the winter, so here's a little spending money. You'll be happy that it was almost at par when I got it.'" He opened the included envelope, pulling out five hundred dollars in United Stated currency.

"You can't get that at par today," Ron quipped. "Though I guess it hasn't gone up in value quite as much as Heather's Tesla stock."

"It's the thought that counts," Mark replied. "We're past taking the kids to Florida, but Patty and I will put this to good use in South Carolina in February." He grinned and shoved the cash in his pocket. Standing the card up, he brought the gift toward him. Making quick work of the paper wrap, he held up a picture of him, his wife Patty, and Mary. They stood in front of the billboard-style sign that he'd erected in front of the subdivision that he'd saved with the money Mary had loaned him. The sign proudly boasted 'Montgomery Homes – A Tradition of Quality'. "Man, I repaid her the money, but I could never repay her for what it meant to me. This is the perfect reminder." The big contractor used the back of his hand to try to brush away a tear without the others noticing.

Ron sat in front of the box. He leaned forward and grabbed his card and gift. The cover of his card showed an apartment tastefully decorated for Christmas. He cleared his throat, then read. "'Dear Ron, you were always the best dressed of my brothers, not that you had a lot of competition with Mark in his overalls and Kevin in his plaid.'" He paused to smirk at his brothers. "'I know your secret though – Sharon picked out most of your clothes. She's got an eye for style. You make sure you give this gift to her. That way it will be put to good use'." He opened the included envelope, holding up a five hundred dollar gift card to Moores Clothing for Men. "I can always use a new suit. If I'd opened this in 2014, it likely would have gotten me two suits."

"Yeah, but they'd be out of style by now," Heather added.

"Good point," Ron replied. "Don't get me wrong, I'm not complaining. This is a great gift that I'll put to use." He smiled, holding up his wrapped present. "Another picture, by the looks of it." He tore the paper, examining the picture before he shared it. A big grin crossed his face.

"You going to share, little brother?" Kevin asked.

Ron held up the photo. "It's a picture of Mary, Sharon, and me in front of the first sign for Sharon's Fabulous Interiors. It's perfect." He passed the photo to Heather.

"And now, last but not least." Kevin stood, carefully reaching into the box to avoid any remaining dust on the outside. His Christmas card showed a snowy log cabin scene. Strangely, it very closely resembled his current home, which Mary had never lived to see. His gut wrenched . He read the inside of the card. "'Dear Kev, as the closest in age to me, I always felt we had a special bond. Perhaps it was our shared responsibility over the other kids when they were young. I kicked around different ideas for you, like movie passes or airline tickets to see Mom. I finally settled on cash. You can likely invest this and turn it into a lot more money.'" Kevin grinned, pulling cash out of the included envelope. "She's right. If I'd opened it in 2014 I could have turned it into a lot more money by now."

"If you'd invested in real estate," quipped a biased Ron.

"You're right. It doesn't matter though. I'll put it in the grandkids' school accounts to give them a boost," Kevin stated. He picked up the fifteen centimetre square box from Mary, obviously not a picture frame. Unwrapping the box, he opened it to find another box – one of those velvet boxes used for travel ornaments. He carefully

189

flipped back the clasp to remove the ball inside. On the ornament was the same house as on the card – his house. Below the house was written 'Kevin's Castle'.

"How …" He sat puzzled. "She never saw my home…"

"Mary had visions," Heather told him. "I don't know how she knew some of the stuff she knew."

"I almost forgot," Kevin replied. "There's another present at the bottom for Mom."

"You should open it," Heather stated to Kevin. "You're the oldest. The oldest remaining."

"I don't know," Kevin questioned. "Maybe we should wait for Mom to get better."

As the siblings debated, Maura's phone rang.

"Doctor Raymond?" she answered, a look of fear on her face.

December 25th
Christmas Day

31 Surprise Call

"I'm going to put you on speaker," Maura told Dr. Raymond. "All of Lizzie's children are here with me." She tapped the speaker phone button as they gathered closer.

"Can you hear me?" the doctor asked.

"Yes, we can. Merry Christmas," Maura responded.

"Merry Christmas to you all as well. I'll cut to the chase."

Maura looked over at Lizzie, still resting, seemingly comfortably. Her intravenous bottle still showed half full. No reason to worry just yet.

The doctor continued. "I have good news for you. Lizzie became responsive late last night. We saw minor movement in her fingers and toes."

The family looked over at their mother, lying motionless on the gurney.

Kevin stammered. "Oh, yes. That is great news." He looked at the others, puzzlement plastered on his slightly pudgy face.

"Yes, it's a sign she's on the mend. If you come up today to visit, she's in a new room now. Seven twelve, I believe." He paused to confirm. "Yes, seven twelve."

"Thank you, Doctor," Kevin replied. "May I ask when she was moved?" He hesitated, then coughed. "We sent flowers this morning to her old room."

"She was moved just after midnight last night. Well, technically this morning. I'll leave a note with the nurse to move the flowers when they come."

Looks of panic spread like wildfire across the stunned faces in the Montgomery living room. Kevin gestured frantically, before realizing he better say something, anything, before the doctor questioned the silence. "Thank you very much, Doctor," he blurted out, rather loudly.

Heather shushed him, making a 'lower' motion with her hand.

Kevin nodded, then with a lower voice added, "I, uh want to say on behalf of the family, thank you for what you've done so far."

"You're welcome. Is Maura still there?"

"I am," she replied.

"If you have any questions, I may not be available. I've got to run down another issue. Some London doctor had another one of my patients transferred early this morning without my permission. When I get my hands on this doctor, he's going to regret it. Just wish I could read his name. Monty P something. Damn doctors can't sign legibly."

"Thank you, Doctor. I'll talk to the duty nurse if I have questions," Maura replied.

The phone went dead.

Silence gripped the room. The group stared at each other, then at the woman they thought was their mother, but obviously was not. One by one they turned to Ron, the man behind the genius plan.

"What?" He straightened up. "We all agreed to it. Some maybe more than others, but we all went through with it."

"Monty P?" Kevin asked. "Did you really sign the doctor's name as Monty Python?"

"It was the first thing that came to my mind," Ron answered. "Tom told me to write anything so long as it looked like a name. I figured what's it matter? We'd planned to have her back in a few minutes by the original plan. Even getting back in a few hours, nobody would have been the wiser."

"What are we going to do!" Heather worried out loud.

Ron began pacing, a habit he shared with Mark. Pacing was his thinking ritual. He found it the best way to clear his head. His best creative moments came pacing in his office or at a property before potential buyers arrived.

Maura fidgeted with the corner of the blanket covering Lizzie. Well, not Lizzie. Covering somebody. She'd always had fidgety hands. Her mother had called it 'dedos nervosos' – nervous fingers.

Kevin tugged slowly on his beard, like he was going to magically pull a solution out of the greying whiskers. His little habit had betrayed him a few times during poker games as his friends all knew his 'tell'.

"We have to return her ASAP," Mark replied, confident in his suggestion. "I shudder to think that somebody else is fretting to understand why their mother got transported to London, well our house actually, early on Christmas morning."

"I'll get Tom on the phone," Ron replied, momentarily stopping his pacing. "He'll know what to do, provided he doesn't kill me."

Dale J. Moore

December 25th
Christmas Day

32 Return

Tom stood at the door, laughing. Not the reaction that Ron had expected from his old friend.

"I didn't think that snatching the wrong person from the hospital would be funny to you," Ron stated, looking behind Tom to see the transport truck with the back doors fully opened.

"Oh, I don't find that funny at all."

"Then why are you laughing?"

"I'm just thinking of what this is going to cost you. Like maybe a sub-prime mortgage." Tom grinned ear to ear.

"You certainly know how to negotiate from a position of strength," Ron grinned back. "One year sub-prime."

"Five"

"Three"

"Deal," Tom reached out a hand. "Three years sub-prime".

Ron shook his hand. "Now I remember why I quit playing poker with you."

Tom grinned at Ron's comment, then became serious. "Do you have any idea yet who we absconded with this morning?"

"The doctor didn't say," Ron sighed, "and we were not about to ask and implicate ourselves in her disappearance."

"It would be nice to know, but at least we know where to return her." Tom placed a hand firmly on Ron's shoulder. "I've got a plan. It's going to take all your family though to pull it off."

"That shouldn't be a problem," Ron nodded. "We're all into this up to our necks. We all need to go to the hospital to see my mom anyway. My real mom, that is. Mary left a present for Mom that's been unopened for ten years. Mom was waiting until we were all together." He shook his head. "Who knows when that may happen again? Mom's not a spring chicken anymore. Hell, none of us are!"

"A present from the grave, eh?" Tom raised an eyebrow. "Very mysterious sounding."

"Mary left presents for all of us. Pretty heavy stuff going through them, for sure." Ron nodded his head and sighed. "We opened the gifts because we thought our mother was with us. We were about to open hers when the doctor called."

"Must have been a shock to find out you snatched the wrong person."

"Major understatement. We were gripped with shock and fear of what may happen to us. I think this heist falls into the category of kidnapping."

Ron opened the double front doors of the house. The remainder of the Montgomery children stood surrounding the gurney of the unknown woman. Tom entered the home, taking his place at the head of the gurney.

"Let's do this," Tom said, looking around.

Kevin and Mark collapsed the gurney, lifted it slowly, and carefully proceeded down the few steps to the driveway.

"Hold it here, guys," Tom ordered the men, just short of the back door of the transport. "I've got to make sure the spare gurney is still out of the way." Tom jumped into the back of the transport, pushing against a second gurney leaning against the one wall. "Okay, you're good," Tom called out, motioning for the occupied gurney to get raised into the vehicle. Tom locked the woman's cart in place.

With one of the benches blocked by the second gurney, Heather started toward the front to jump in the cab with Tom.

"Heather, you need to go in the back. Ron can come up front with me. I'll explain the plan on the drive."

Kevin tossed Ron a transport jacket to put on in the front seat. Tom talked through the plan a couple of times on the drive to the hospital, giving each person a role in the play that was about to unfold. A play founded in misdirection.

Stopping in the hospital loading zone, Tom began to direct his actors. Ron and Mark unloaded the patient from the transport, rolling her toward the doors. Tom jumped into the back to flip the empty gurney upright. During the ride, Kevin and Mark had wrapped Heather in bandages, similar to the unknown patient on the gurney. A reluctant mummified Heather lay down.

"Remember not to say anything," instructed Tom. "Don't even groan if the boys drop you."

"Funny," she replied, followed by her fingers pretending to zip her lips.

"That's it," Tom told her, loosely strapping her down. Aside from her head, her body was covered with blankets. He hooked up an intravenous pole holding a mostly empty bag whose tube ran under the blanket where Heather held it in her hand.

Heather didn't like this part of the plan one bit. She felt helpless and if things went sideways, she didn't know how quickly she could get the restraints off to make a run for it. She knew, however, that it had to be her on the gurney. Tom thought the body on the bed should be close in size to their patient; the guys were all too big.

Kevin and Tom unloaded Heather from the truck and raised her bed. Tom slammed the truck's back doors shut then they rolled Heather to join the others waiting inside.

The teams switched places, with Ron and Mark in charge of maneuvering Heather. Tom and Kevin guided the gurney of the unknown patient. The Montgomery children waited nervously for the large, restricted-access elevator. It felt like an eternity to the Montgomery clan. Like watching a pot of water, hoping it would boil faster.

Tom calmed them during the two minutes the wait took, talking about his Christmas morning and what he got his wife.

When the elevator arrived, the group held back while another patient was rolled out. All of them but Tom kept their heads down, trying to avoid eye contact and recognition later. Both gurneys were squeezed in, and the seventh floor button pushed.

"Ready?" Tom asked.

Ron, Kevin, and Mark nodded. They pulled their baseball caps down even more to obscure their faces as much as possible.

"How about you, Queen Hatshepsut?" Tom asked Heather.

A thumbs-up came from under the blanket.

"Queen who?" Ron asked.

"She was an Egyptian mummy." Tom looked at Ron. "Never mind."

"I'm more concerned with finding *our* mommy," Ron smirked.

The elevator ding announced their arrival. Tom motioned to Ron. "If you get stopped, just bullshit your way out of it. You're a salesman, should be a piece of cake for you."

Ron grinned back, then nodding at Mark, they pushed Heather into the hallway. They stopped before the corner with the nurses' station, looking back at the others. Tom and Kevin had exited the elevator and waited there. Tom motioned Ron to proceed.

Ron and Mark rolled Heather past the nurses' station, slowly enough to get noticed, but quick enough to pretend they didn't hear the nurse.

"Hey, you need to check in here!" A female nurse leaned over the counter watching the bed roll away. "Stop!" she hollered, frantically waving her hands to get their attention.

The crew ignored her calls, continuing to the farthest hallway, away from the corridor with room seven hundred and seven.

When the transport crew kept moving, the nurse motioned to the male nurse behind her. The two nurses scampered out of the nurses' station in pursuit of the bed.

With the sight of the two nurses running after Heather's bed, Tom and Kevin quickly rolled past the station towards room seven hundred and seven. To their surprise, when they got to the room, another occupant had moved in.

"Shit!" Tom muttered, rubbing his chin to think. "I thought they'd hold the room for the woman to return from London."

"Let's just leave her here," Kevin offered, a flicker of panic in his eyes, worried the whole plan was about to implode.

"We can't. She's on my gurney." Tom's eyes darted around for a solution. "You stay here. I'll try to find an unoccupied room. Play dumb if anyone comes in the room. Just say you're waiting for your boss to give you orders."

Kevin nodded and Tom flew out of the room.

In the next corridor, Ron tapped Heather on the leg, her signal to get up. She sat up as the gurney continued progressing away from the nurses' station. She moved the right handrail down and out of the way. Heather clutched the left rail as the bed still rolled down the hallway.

"Get ready," Ron told her.

She nodded. The bed came to a rattling halt. Heather lurched for a second, then jumped off. Ron pushed the empty bed sending it further down the hallway. Kevin and Heather disappeared into the nearest patient's room. Ron followed, closing the door mostly behind him. Ron could hear the two nurses run right past their room.

"Quickly, guys. They'll loop back." Ron motioned to the others. He and Kevin tugged to remove their transport jackets and stuff them into a large empty Christmas gift sack they'd brought – one that could hold a bunch of large presents, like Santa's bag. Heather ripped at the tensor bandages wrapping her face, shoving them into the garbage by the bathroom door. She stuffed handfuls of bunched-up paper towels on top of her garbage, obscuring it from view. The three of them took their places in front of the hospital bed in the room, like visitors to the unconscious patient.

The male nurse ducked his head in the room.

"Did you see a transport crew?"

The pretend-grieving trio slowly turned. Ron held his finger to his mouth with a 'shhhh' sound.

The nurse apologized and left.

Tom meanwhile had located another room with an empty bed.

"It's risky," Tom stated. "It's back near the nurses' station."

Kevin's face showed his concern. "Do we have a choice?"

"Not really," Tom flatly replied. "Ready?"

Kevin sighed and nodded.

Tom stuck his head out the door. All clear. They pushed the gurney into the hallway and straightened it out. Tom glanced behind him. "Third room on the right," Tom pointed as he whispered to an anxious Kevin.

"Stop right there!" The female nurse called to them from behind.

Tom paused. He hoped he knew the nurse to make this easier. He turned and breathed a sigh of relief. "Sandy, how are you doing?"

"Not good right now, Tom. Did you see another gurney go by?"

"No," he calmly replied. "Just this one."

"What room is that for?" the nurse asked.

"I thought it was for seven hundred and seven, but there's another bed in there."

"Hmm," the nurse replied. "Can you give me the paperwork?"

Ron handed over the clipboard. "Here's the issue, Sandy." He looked her in the eye, grinning sheepishly. "She is a return from last night. I got all the way to London and had to turn back."

"What?" Sandy asked, startled.

"Yeah, they didn't want her. I showed them the paperwork and they laughed at me."

The nurse stood, puzzled.

"It seems my dispatcher found this on the floor last night and thought it fell off the printer. She sent it to me, and I blindly followed the instructions."

"I'm confused," the nurse admitted.

Kevin stood silently, unaware of this plot twist in their play.

"I'm such an idiot." Tom pointed to the top of the paperwork. "See the date?"

The nurse pulled the form closer. She read it aloud. "Twelve twenty four." She looked at Tom. "What's wrong with that?"

"Look closer," he implored her.

She stared at it. "Oh, now I see it. It says ten twenty four." She looked at Tom. "Boy, that looks like a twelve."

"Right, eh? Man, I just wasted six hours going back and forth, not to mention arguing with London." He paused. "Where should I put her, since the room we took her from is occupied."

"Oh yes, let's see." She looked down the hallway. "Up here on the right. Seven hundred and one is empty."

"Much obliged," Tom tipped his hat and grinned.

The nurse followed them into the room to watch the transfer. Once completed, she signed the form acknowledging receipt of the patient. Tom and Kevin took the empty gurney and left. The elevator doors closed behind them, Kevin let out a huge sigh that seemed to come from his entire body.

"That was exciting!" Kevin stammered, holding his rapidly beating heart. "Scary but exhilarating at the same time. Man, remind me never to play poker with you," he blurted, still breathing faster than healthy for a man his age.

Tom laughed. "Ron learned that lesson a long time ago."

The doors opened to the ground floor, revealing the other three actors in the play. The same signs of relief covered the faces of the other Montgomerys. The group exchanged fist bumps in a minor celebration.

"Can we get out of here now?" Heather asked, rubbing at her face. "My skin is itchy from those bandages. It feels like I've got a rash all over my face. I probably look contagious!"

"It's not that bad," Ron replied, before laughing.

"Great," Heather moaned.

Tom grabbed Ron's hat from his head and plopped it on Heather's head, pulling down the brim. "There," he smiled at Heather. "Fixed."

Ron pulled his hood over his head.

"You guys can head to my truck with this bed and wait there," Tom told them. "I've got to retrieve that other gurney."

They nodded, leaving Tom waiting for the elevator to return.

Arriving back on the seventh floor, Tom approached the nurses' station. He was happy to see Sandy sitting there.

"Man am I having a bad day!" he told the nurse.

"Did you lose a patient or something?" she laughed.

"Not quite, but close," Tom panted for effect. "I got a dispatch on my way to the truck. Seems that someone stole one of my gurneys. Likely took it for a joy ride. My other crew is going floor by floor looking for it. I told them I'd cover seven and up." He lifted his hands into prayer position in front of his chin. He pleaded, "Any chance you've seen my runaway bed?"

Her face lit up with eyes wide. "That explains it! A bed went racing by here about thirty minutes ago. Peter," she motioned behind her, "and I chased them. All we found was the empty bed. I wish we'd caught those kids!"

"You know where it is!" Tom enthusiastically opened his arms wide. "That's great. You just saved me an hour of searching floors! Can you show me?"

"Sure, follow me," Sandy grinned, happy she'd been able to help.

Tom followed her down the far corridor. Reaching the gurney, he bent down to confirm the 'property of' tag. "That's it. Thanks, I can call off the search on the other floors. I owe you a coffee and donut."

She laughed. "You can skip the donut," she held her hands on her hips. "After the holidays, last thing I need is more carbs."

Tom patted his stomach. "Don't I know that!" He put his hands on the gurney. "Thanks again." He picked up his phone. "Got to call my guys."

She took the hint and left.

He pretended to talk to someone, then rolled the bed past the nurses' station and into the elevator. As the elevator door closed in front of his face, he smiled at his distorted reflection staring back from the steel door. *That was a good plan, Tom, my boy. Good plan.*

Dale J. Moore

December 25ᵗʰ
Christmas Day

33 *Maura's Visit*

With the excitement of returning the unknown patient, the Montgomery children agreed they needed to head home and unwind before visiting their mother. They also didn't want to risk getting recognized for their earlier caper; they'd need to change their clothes.

The transport truck rocked with loud voices and laughter. The crew exchanged their stories, fears, and close calls. Heather applied some cream she found in Tom's supplies to her reddening face. Mark joked that tomatoes were out of season unless she was from a Leamington greenhouse. Kevin went on about the brilliance of Tom's verbal maneuvering when they were caught in the hallway by Nurse Sandy. Exiting the vehicle in their mother's driveway, they thanked Tom for his help.

"I have to say this is not how I expected Christmas Day to go," Tom smiled at the group. "It's been a Christmas I will never forget, that's for sure." He looked at Ron. "Are you forgetting something, Ron?"

Ron wrote on the back of a business card and grunted as he handed it over to Tom.

Tom read it, "'Sub-prime mortgage for three years', music to my wallet." He leaned forward and gave his friend a hug. "Merry Christmas, Ron. Don't wait so long to visit again. Got it?"

Ron nodded. "Thanks for everything. You saved our collective skins today."

"Maybe I should have held out for five years," Tom teased.

"Get out of here," Ron laughed, smacking his friend's shoulder.

The group watched Tom close the back of the truck and leave.

The chatter grew loud as the Montgomery children poured back into their mother's home. The noisy voices and laughing alerted Maura to their return.

"Oh good, you're back," Maura grinned, wiping her hands on her apron. "That means none of you got arrested on Christmas Day. That's a relief. I would have hated to think of you sharing a cell with Mr. Miller."

They laughed.

"At least I could have executed Plan B," Kevin replied in reference to the brothers beating up Danny.

"Did you see your mother?" Maura asked.

"No, we just wanted to get out of there without anybody in handcuffs," chuckled Kevin.

"We're going to grab a snack and head up in a few hours," Heather added.

"Good. Do you mind watching the turkey? I want to go see your mother and wish her a Merry Christmas."

"Sure, let's go to the kitchen. You can tell Kevin and I what we need to do," Heather replied, smiling. "I think we're the two cooks in the family. Sharon and Patty spoil Ron and Mark."

With Maura leading the way, Heather tugged on Maura's apron strings from behind. Maura turned, surprised, then laughed.

Returning from the kitchen, Kevin spoke to his brothers. "Well, I'm going to crash for a few hours." He looked at his watch. "There's really nothing to do in the kitchen for a while. Heather said she's staying up to read in the living room. She'll peek in on the food every so often, just in case."

"Napping sounds like a plan." Ron held his head. "I don't know if I have a bit of a hangover from drinking too much last night or a headache from the adrenalin rush of our caper."

"Caper. I like the sound of that," Mark replied. "Our own little Christmas caper. I'm going to hit the hay too."

Maura carried a small Christmas plant up to Lizzie's room. She had not previously brought cards or decorations for the holidays, or the photo with Lizzie's late husband. The doctor had talked about her boss moving rooms as her treatment changed, but Maura hadn't expected the move to take place so soon, on Christmas Eve/morning. Maura wished to cheer up the drab hospital room with its bland cream coloured walls. A bit of green with a red ribbon would do the trick.

Entering the room, Maura could not tell much difference from the last visit. A small vase of flowers sat on the bedside table. They must have moved Mark's bouquet from the old room this morning. She couldn't tell any difference from the mystery woman the children had brought home. Maura sat at the hospital bedside, fidgeting with her restless fingers. She finally thought of something to talk about.

"You" — she cleared her throat and corrected herself, — "*We* won't have to worry about that creep Danny Miller anymore. Your children took care of that." She didn't mention her key role. "You can use that money for something better, like maybe more inflatable Christmas decorations for the front lawn." She laughed to herself, knowing the lawn could barely hold any more. Maura stood up and removed her uncomfortable, and becoming hot, coat. She thought hospital rooms were always stuffy and warm. She moaned to herself.

"Or better yet, you can buy me a car, like the one Kevin almost bought for me. But one that works." She smiled at her boss. "Okay, that sounds a little greedy. Maybe just a small raise." She paused to hold Lizzie's arm. She caressed her employer's skin, hoping it provided some comfort from the pain. "That's right, I'm sticking around. I changed my mind. I realize how much you need me. It would be selfish of me to quit. Especially now." A tear crawled down her cheek and dropped gently onto a bare section of Lizzie's arm.

Lizzie's arm twitched.

December 25th
Christmas Day

34   Mary's Final Gift

Maura returned to the Montgomery home, excitedly telling the kids about the slight movement in their mother's arm. It raised the spirits of everyone in advance of their visit. Maura told them Christmas dinner would be ready around five-thirty, asking if they could complete their visit and return by then. They said that should work. Heather assured her that she had Maura's phone number if they were running late.

Ron drove the group downtown in his Cadillac, the heaters on for the leather seats.

Heather held Mary's gift on her lap. "Any guesses? It's kind of heavy."

"We almost all got picture frames," Mark responded. "It's too heavy for wood by the sound of it. I'm going to go with a ceramic picture frame in pastel colours. Butterflies or rainbows around the edges. The picture is all of us at Mary's wedding."

"Can't you be more specific?" Heather laughed. "I think she's only got a copy in a photo album. That would be a wonderful present for Mom to display on the mantle, provided Danny Miller is photoshopped out of it. Anybody else hazard a guess?"

"A Bible with gold trimmed pages. Knowing Mary's connections, it's signed by God himself." Kevin paused. "Or God herself," he winked to Heather.

"My guess is it's a signed manuscript of her last book," Ron chimed in from the front seat. "She always signed one and the publisher didn't remember receiving one for that book. That would be worth a bit of money now."

"What about you, Heather?" Kevin asked. "What do you think it is?"

"I really have no idea," she said, thinking for a moment. "Whatever it is, I'm sure it will be personal for Mom." She clasped the package tighter. "I like Mark's idea best. A picture like that would warm Mom's heart, that's for sure."

Inside their mother's hospital room, they individually greeted her with Merry Christmas wishes then encircled the bed. Mark nudged the intravenous pole out of the way to stand closer to his mother, and to avoid setting off another alarm.

"Did you see that?" Heather excitedly asked the others. "She moved her fingers."

"She just turned her head a bit too," Kevin replied. "Shhhh." He held up his arms. "I think she's trying to say something." He leaned in real close, feeling her breath warm his cheek. The room fell silent. After a few seconds, her head turned back away from her son.

"Well?" Ron asked. "What did she say?"

Kevin straightened up. "It was hard to make out. I think she said two things. I think the first one was 'not Maura's fault'. The second phrase sounded like 'love you all'." He paused briefly, "'except Ron'."

The others laughed, except Ron, who punched Kevin in the arm. "She did not, you idiot."

"Mom, it's me, Heather." She gently placed her hand on her mother's arm, between the bandages covering her upper body and hands. "We found a gift Mary left you."

Their mother's chest moved up and down, like she gasped. They all saw it.

Kevin nodded to Heather to continue. "Mary left each of us a gift to open the year after she passed." She cleared her throat. "Obviously we missed that, but we're all together now so we opened our gifts at home." She slowly caressed her mother's arm as she spoke. "We're going to open the family card then your present, since we are all together and don't know when that will happen again." She stared into her mother's eyes, looking for some acknowledgement. Heather swore she saw a small tear crawl down her mother's cheek and down under the bandages around her eyes.

"I think we are good to go," whispered Mark.

Kevin and Ron nodded.

"Here goes," Heather said with a huge exhale. She tore open the envelope to reveal a custom card. The cover was a picture of their home when they were kids. She showed it to her mother, then to the others. A letter fell from the card onto the bed.

Kevin picked up the letter and grasped it firmly.

Heather read the inside of the card. 'To the best mother ever! Thanks for always being there for me, especially for the difficult days near the end. Love, Mary.'

Heather wiped her eyes. She looked at Kevin. "Can you read the letter, please?" She sobbed, snagging a handful of tissues to wipe her face.

"Sure," Kevin replied, placing his arm around his sister for comfort. He unfolded the letter with his free hand. "Here goes. 'Mom, I already sealed the other cards, so I'm including this letter here for Kevin, Ron, Mark, and Heather.'" Kevin turned his gaze temporarily away from his mother and toward his siblings. "'I'm hoping everyone has come back home to spend this Christmas with Mom. While I'm sure the last Christmas was rough on all of you due to my untimely demise, none of you lost a daughter. And while we lost our father near Christmas, she lost her life partner – keep that in mind. She really needs the love of her family now, more so than any other time of year.'" Kevin paused, removing his arm from around his sister to grab a tissue and blow his nose. "Sorry, guys." He continued. "'We had some truly memorable Christmases as a family. I hope you cherish them as much as I did. I hope you remain present and strong for Mom during the holidays, even if you take turns visiting as your young families continue to grow. Do this for me, please. Love you and miss you all!'" Kevin turned the page over to reveal a blank page. "That's it," he proclaimed, looking at red eyes all around.

"Man do I feel like shit," Ron stated.

He felt a mild tap on his hand. It was his mother. He laugh-cried. "Sorry, Mom." He looked at the others. "I guess she can hear what we're saying."

"I'm opening the gift now," Heather said, looking at her mother. She pulled open the one end to reveal another envelope.

Mark motioned to her. She passed the pink envelope to him. He tore it open to read the letter inside.

"'Mom, they say that great artists and authors are never truly appreciated until they die. Well, here's to hoping that's the case and this final book of mine makes enough money for you to fund your grandchildren's tuition.'"

Kevin interrupted. "Her existing books have already done that!"

Mark smiled. "And great grandchildren," he added. He continued with the letter. "'If that happens, use the rest for the charity of your choice. Something to save the planet would suit me, but there are many groups in need. I'll leave it to you to decide. Love you forever, your daughter Mary.'"

"The back," Ron pointed to the letter. "There's writing on the back."

"Oh, yeah, thanks," Mark nodded. "There's a P.S. It says 'P.S. This is a work of fiction that has very much been inspired by my wonderful family. Some of my favourite moments make up the backbone of this story. You'll no doubt see parts of each other in the characters. Just remember, it's fiction. Love, Mary.'"

Heather pulled out the manuscript. A thumb drive fell onto the bed, which Kevin scooped up and placed in his pocket. The book slid out of the package upside down. Mary flipped it over to read the title to herself before sharing. With trembling hands and reddening eyes, she looked at her siblings, and then her mother. She read the cover. "The Last Christmas: A Story of Family."

The End

A Small Favour

I hope you enjoyed The Last Christmas. Can I ask a small favour?

Leaving a review helps authors, especially independent authors like me!

I appreciate every honest review of my work. It only takes a few minutes – it doesn't need to be an eloquent composition, just a few thoughts will help incredibly! Posting to Amazon or any book site would be appreciated.

Thanks for your time!

Dale J. Moore

Other Novels by Dale J. Moore

Trials of Katrina Series – Cozy Mystery / Amateur Sleuth

Book 2: Friends of the Deceased

How does a small town girl end up investigating crime at a funeral home in Toronto? Drop-dead gorgeous Katrina is trying to run her new salon and take her relationship to a new level. The unexpected death of a client and struggles with her salon lead her to the Shady Rest funeral home.

As she stumbles her way through the personal problems that plague her world, Katrina ends up immersed in the world of preparing people for the next world.

With the help of a ruggedly handsome police detective, some old friends, and a few new ones, will she get to the bottom of what's going on, or end up buried by it? One thing is certain; when Katrina gets involved, chaos and comedy will ensue.

Book 3: Days of Wine and Tomatoes

Katrina is back for her third chaotic adventure! Trying to revive a struggling relationship with her detective boyfriend, they're off for a long weekend to wine country along the shores of Lake Erie. Customary to Katrina's exploits, trouble crosses her path like a black cat, altering the idyllic getaway.

As the town of Leamington holds its annual Tomato Fest, the summer waterfront party atmosphere is disrupted by a kidnapping. Mixing the enjoyment of the lake front wineries with sleuthing and rooting out clues, Katrina missteps from one mishap to another while solving mysteries in her unique way.

Having been the Life of the Party, and after surviving Friends of the Deceased, Katrina's latest escapade has barrels of wine and laughs. Mix in a bushel of tomatoes, a misfit crew, and the summer sun, and you've got Days of Wine and Tomatoes.

Thrillers

<u>Ubiquitous Medical</u>

UbiquiMed: We're Everywhere, For You!

A brilliant researcher isolated in search of a cure.
The star of a media parody broadcast with a favourite target.
A young couple with decisions to make about their children's future.
The corporate executive driven by his vision.
Such is the influence of Ubiquitous Medical.

"UBIQUITOUS MEDICAL is a fast paced ride that will keep you guessing. Twists and turns keep you on the edge of your seat, while the characters grow and deepen with every page. Dale J. Moore's voice shines through in this unique tale of a chilling future." **Gemma Halliday, award winning author of the High Heels Mysteries**

Amends

If life gave you a death-defying wake-up call, would you sit back counting
your blessings or realize you'd been given a second chance?

Dr. Tre Brightman seems to have it all. A young dentist with a Hollywood clientele and movie star relationships, he's living the high life. A fatal tragedy leaves him seriously injured and drives him to evaluate his actions and the casualties he's left along the side of his road to success.

He embarks on a cross-country journey of atonement, unaware that one of those victims is determined to resolve their past conflict – permanently. Tre's quest devolves into a physical and psychological battle of endurance leaving him to wonder if he'll survive to make Amends.

Benjay and the Magical Bubbles Series

Middle Grade Fantasy

A Story of Wonder : Book One

A boy and his family, magical creatures with special abilities, and environmental crooks.

What if your new best friend was a Bubble – one that talked and flew? How would you get anyone, especially your parents, to believe you?
Seven-year-old Benjay Marshall wishes people treated him normally. He feels normal; he's just missing part of his leg after dealing with cancer. Fueled by an overactive imagination and a humourous way of expressing himself, Benjay's life takes an extraordinary turn due to a chance encounter with a magical Bubble. As he learns more about the Bubbles, the more he realizes his family will think he's simply spinning another tall tale.

With his father in grave danger from crooks sabotaging his environmental project, how does Benjay make his family trust that Bubbles are not only real, but are possibly the *only* chance to save the day?

Danger at Christmas: Book Two

A human boy, a magical Bubble girl, and lives in danger! How far would *you* go to save someone close?

Eight-year-old Benjay Marshall is back for another adventure with the Bubbles!

Having missed Christmas battling cancer the past two years, Benjay is excited to celebrate all the holiday traditions with his family. Happy Christmas activities take a perilous turn with a robbery at the century-old bank where Benjay's mother works.

Benjay's new Bubble friend Peepers has a terrible feeling that her human friend is in danger. Her fears intensify with the ominous vision from a visiting Elder. With a secret motive, the Bubble Elders launch a mission to verify the vision. Peepers and her older brother Fret leave to investigate the curious vision, not knowing the danger they will encounter. All they know are their orders: keep Benjay safe.

Stopping the robbers seems like a monumental task for an eight-year-old boy with a prosthetic leg and his clever twelve-year-old sister. Can Benjay and Lindsay foil the robbery? Can they rescue their mother? Will the Bubbles be able to help?

Bubbles 2: Danger at Christmas juggles suspense and humour, with the usual dose of mayhem for Benjay and the Bubbles. Sure to be enjoyed by both boys and girls.

Benjay's Battle: Book Three

A devious doctor, a secret laboratory, and a boy in a fight against time. And of course, magical Bubbles!

Benjay faces the biggest challenge of his young life. His magical Bubble friend Peepers has no idea of the danger that lies ahead as she breaks the rules to help her human friend. It's the kind of danger that could impact all Bubbles. Mysterious events unfold, including unexplained improvements in Benjay's condition and strange dreams of a woman who may be more than she appears. Join Benjay and Peepers as they face peril in their latest magical adventure!

Benjay's Battle is a fast-paced adventure that blends elements of fantasy, science fiction, and mystery while exploring themes of friendship, curiosity, and hope in the face of adversity.

Bubbles on the Run: Book Four

Magical Bubbles have existed on earth in a hidden civilization that secretly coexists alongside humanity, usually only intervening to prevent catastrophe. When two Bubbles are tagged with human tracking devices, they must flee pursuing federal agents and avoid capture at all costs. As the human agents close in, the intelligent creatures fear becoming laboratory specimens – and worse, exposure and exploitation of all Bubbles around the world.

Driven to repay his debt to the Bubbles for helping him and his family, young cancer survivor Benjay enlists the help of his sister Lindsay and his friend Sarah. Risking everything to protect the magical creatures, they must outsmart agents equipped with advanced technology and dangerous ambitions.

This riveting adventure is ideal for young adults and entertaining for all ages.

Short Stories

Benjay's Halloween: Book 1.1

A missing cat, a broken leg, and scary skeletons!

In this short story, Benjay's excitement for Halloween keeps hitting roadblocks. Will he go trick-or-treating or be stuck at home handing out candy?

A delightful middle-grade short story that captures the magic and excitement of every child's favorite spooky holiday. An entertaining tale blending humor, adventure, and valuable life lessons about resilience and family bonds.

Short Stories
Benjay's Santa Claus Parade: Book 1.2

Runaway inflatables, substitute Santas, and pandemonium at the parade!

When young Benjay spots his neighbor Mr. Guenther mysteriously floating in mid-air, he's certain he's discovered Santa's secret identity. When disaster strikes at the Christmas parade, with Benjay trapped in the middle of it, will Santa save the day? Is Mr. Guenther really Santa Claus or is there an even more magical explanation?

This heartwarming adventure proves that sometimes the best Christmas magic comes from ordinary people doing extraordinary things.

Learning to Write

Young Writer's Workbook

This comprehensive workbook is an engaging and interactive guide designed to nurture young writers from grades 3-8 (ages 8-14). It offers a structured approach to developing writing skills through a series of creative exercises and activities.

Key features:
1. Age-appropriate progression
2. Diverse writing techniques
3. Sensory exploration
4. Character building
5. Creative thinking
6. Practical skills
7. Interactive elements
8. Real-world applications
9. Storytelling techniques
10. Writing prompts

The workbook is an excellent tool for both classroom use and individual learning, providing a solid foundation for aspiring young writers to develop their craft. Its engaging content and gradual skill progression make it an invaluable resource for parents, teachers, and young authors alike.